Music Prod Beginners 2020 Edition

How to Produce Music

The Easy to Read Guide for Music Producers (Music Business, Electronic Dance Music, Edm, Producing Music)

By Tommy Swindali

Discover "How to Find Your Sound"

http://musicprod.ontrapages.com/

Swindali music coaching/Skype lessons.

Email djswindali@gmail.com for info and pricing

Music Production For Beginners 2020 Edition

How to Produce Music

The Easy to Read Guide for Music Producers (Music Business, Electronic Dance Music, Edm, Producing Music)

By Tommy Swindali

Table of Contents

Introduction

What does music production entail? This question must have crossed your mind more than once if you are genuinely interested in producing music. Music production is simply explained as an umbrella term that envelopes the different processes involved in the production of songs.

Since there are different parts of music production, a music producer may be more talented and well established in one aspect of music production than another. For instance, some producers focus on the engineering aspects of music; some focus on the composing aspect, some focus on the business aspects, some focus either on the mentorship aspects or the artistic aspect, while others are just naturally gifted in all aspects. They have the ear for good sound and a natural affinity for producing great music such that anything they touch turns to gold.

Music production involves spending a lot of time listening to already written records, editing the sounds, the rhythm, the beat, the vocals to conform to your taste, creating fresh records from scratch, and remixing already produced and published songs. In simple terms, music production entails; recording, composing, audio mixing, and audio mastering, among others. Do not fret; more light will be shed on the entirety of what it takes to make a song.

Who is a producer? A music producer is an individual with an inborn artistic personality, which he or she utilizes to combine all the necessary tools, techniques, skills, and all other materials required to produce music. A music producer must have the ability to combine all the necessary components to achieve maximum effect. A music producer is akin to a commander of a platoon of soldiers or a director of a film in charge of managing all resources; the artiste, the audio engineers, the songwriter, the sounds, and all other resources required to produce music, in order to efficiently produce music that promises to be a hit.

A music producer doesn't only spend time in the studio making a song or songs, he or she also spends time outside the studio or music room if you like marketing the song. This fulfills the entrepreneurial duty of a producer.

The processes, methods, and technology involved in music production are ever-changing. Music production has been evolving since the existence of music itself, and it will continue to do so. As a result, music production appears daunting and tasking to a beginner. Apart from the ever-changing nature of music production techniques and technologies, the production cost is also another obstacle for a beginner. Despite the fact that the nature of the expenses has changed over time, music production still requires a significant budget. It is a relief that the days when you have to rent a studio space or purchase enormous space-consuming types of equipment to be able to record a song are gone. All the requirements for music production in recent times are easy to get; a laptop, free software, and a good internet connection. This has made music production relatively easier to achieve compared to the old times whereby music could only be heard on the radio, at concerts, in clubs. This fact does not only culminate as an advantage in the form of making music production easier, but it also brings about a disadvantage in the form of fierce competition present in the industry.

This is why, as a rookie in music production, it is not advisable for you to waste your time and energy on half-baked forums or YouTube videos. What you need to become an authority are the right tools, commitment, passion, hard work, diverse skills, an efficient marketing strategy, and oftentimes money. Furthermore, it is not until you attend music classes or study music encyclopedias before you can produce music. In fact, you do not need a strong musical background or a very sophisticated technology to produce music. This book tries to show you how you can comfortably produce music with the simplest, most efficient, and most trending set up available.

What you get from the book

The objective of this book is to provide you with the necessary information and to serve as a form of manual for you in your music production journey. The book seeks to teach you techniques on how to harness from the best producer to how to fit your studio space regardless of the size (which may be in your living room, bedroom, basement, a carved out countertop space in your kitchen, or even a bag/box you can carry with you everywhere you go). Furthermore, the book promises producer techniques, software, materials, and equipment that are budget-friendly, especially for a beginner. The book has been particularly designed as a step by step reference book, such that you have to go through from the beginning to the end to get the most out of it. The book promises to give you everything you need to become the best music producer you can be.

What you will not get from the book

Manuals from the manufacturers of varying brands of studio equipment are there to teach you how to operate the equipment. Just so you know, this book will not give you that. This is because the information that will be provided is not specific to any type of software, whether Reaper, Cubase, Ableton Live, Pro tools, or any other Digital Audio Workstation (DAW) software. The information available is general and goes across the board.

Chapter One : The Beginner Recording Studio

In this chapter, we will be outlining all you need to establish your recording studio, how to get the basics that are required and recommended, and the affordability of the whole music recording shebang. As a beginner, it will be irrational for you to spend a lot of money renting studio space to make your tracks. The best course of action is to carve out space in your home for recording activities.

The space you call your home studio depends on you and the available space you can spare. It could be right by your bedside or in a spare room or in your garage if you have one or in the basement. It could even be a portable one that is compatible with travel if you are the type that is always on the move. There are a lot of advantages accrued to you having your own home recording studio. It allows you to have easy access to your gear so that you can work at your own time and in an atmosphere of your own choice, with no disturbances or distractions except for the ones you create yourself.

Don't get it wrong; there are a lot of reasons people go into music production. You could be into it just for fun, or you could be into it to build a career and earn a living. As the saying goes, "anything worth doing is worth doing well," therefore, if you are going to record songs, you should do it with a modicum of seriousness and dedication regardless of the reason for it.

As there are advantages arising from having a home recording studio, there are also disadvantages accrued to it. Having a studio space at home promotes laziness and the tendency to procrastinate. The fact that you do not have to get up from bed every morning, take a shower, dress up, get in your car and drive to the studio kills the drive that stems from having to go out and get things done. If your studio was a distance away from your home and you had to go out to record your song, you would not just arrive at the studio and sit while doing nothing. However, whether these disadvantages are applicable to you is entirely dependent on your level of discipline.

Making your Home Recording Studio a Reality

There are three major factors that dictate the kind of home studio you build; space available to you, your musical requirements, and your budget. These factors have a kind of causal connection such that your budget dictates the type and quantity of equipment you can buy while taking into consideration your musical goals you can plan to achieve. In addition, your home studio space also dictates the type of equipment you can purchase. Therefore, a little research about the equipment and a little self-assessment of your music goals, are very necessary when selecting studio equipment and setting up your home studio. You cannot just walk into a studio shop and pick any equipment just because you like it or whatnot. It is not done. You need to observe due diligence at this point.

Home studios vary from very simple to very sophisticated, from gradually assembled overtime to assembled in one go. However, take note that most big and successful recording studios today were not built in one go; rather, one equipment was added to the bunch gradually over time. Therefore, start small, get the basics, and enter the music-making proper. Then you grow from there because the more you record and gain the much-required experience, the closer you are to making fabulous-sounding recordings. When I say small, I mean you have to prioritize when getting your gear, which may be as simple as a portable digital recorder with a built-in microphone in the corner of your room or even your smartphone with a kick-ass recording app with amazing features, and a pair of headphones.

Steps to Set Up a Home Recording Studio

• Select and prepare the best spot

Choose a spot you feel most comfortable in. Make sure it is the furthest possible from any source of the noise. This is important because noise does not only distort the quality of your recording; it can also pose as a medium of distraction. I have realized it is actually beneficial to demarcate the studio area so that it gives off a different feel from the general feel of the house. Curtains, wooden boards, or any other material that can serve the purpose of a screen can be used. Another important requirement is the flooring and the ceiling. Concrete and tile floors coupled with hardwood ceiling are ideal. However, if these are not attainable, you can lay a thick rug in the studio area or any other material that can absorb noise. All these trimmings are essential because the state of the room plays a big role in the quality of sound produced.

In the spirit of preparing the room, set up a flat surface or a desk or a table very close to a plug power-point in the room. Remove all unnecessary fixings in the room, such as paintings on the wall that can cause unwanted vibrations, furniture that are not needed, and the likes. You can leave other things like shelves, cupboards, curtains in the room. They will serve the purpose of natural acoustic treatment and sound treatment. This helps you manage your budget instead of purchasing sophisticated acoustic and sound treatment installations. However, these acoustic panels and soundproofing panels are not unnecessary as they help to keep outside noise out of and sound recordings within the studio room. They just cost money and, in the process, put additional strain on your already stretched budget.

• Getting your equipment

Now that you have prepared the room/studio space, it is now time to purchase the music production weapons (equipment). The type and caliber of equipment you decide to work with depending on your current finances and current music needs but for the purpose of establishing the essentials regardless of the varying preferences, you need to acquire the following:

- Computer; a laptop, a tab or a desktop

- Sound monitors; at least 2

- Headphones

- A Digital Audio Workstation (DAW) Software

- Microphones

- Audio interface/Sound card

- Optional studio props; Music instruments Digital interface (MIDI for short) keyboard, studio monitor stands, cables, Mic stands, and pop filters.

The Computer

For someone who is just starting out, if you already have a computer good enough for audio recordings then, all the sweeter. However, if you do not have one, you will have to purchase one with the right specs to get the job done. Do not worry; you will be well acquainted with the perfect specs for audio recording shortly. I suggest you buy a computer that you will be able to dedicate solely to the audio recording because running other applications on it may affect its recording output. If you can only lay hands on a laptop, it is all good; you can make it work with other supporting gear. However, for great efficiency, a desktop, whether a Macintosh (MAC for short) brand or a PC brand, is preferable. Notwithstanding the fact that there have been arguments in the home audio recording community about the better of the two computers in the past, it is your personal preference that should prevail. Most well-established home recording studios opt for a MAC because they believed PC computers crash easily and have too many bugs for audio recording without incident. It is my joy to inform you that this mentality is no more tenable. What is now tenable is the smooth compatibility between the computer system and the recording software of your choice.

Selecting a computer should not only depend on your preference. Your preference must reflect the required specs for optimum audio recording. Therefore, the computer type you buy or decide to install in your home studio must have the following specs:

• Processor (CPU); the speed of your computer's processor determines how well your chosen audio software runs on it.

So try to get the fastest processor you can afford. Note that the barest minimum is a dual-core processor. Therefore it is recommended that you try as much as possible to get a 2.8GHZ dual-core processor at least for a good result and a 3 GHz dual-core processor for a much better audio recording experience if you are going for a laptop, but if you are going for a desktop, a quad-core processor is ideal. The higher you go, the better.

• Memory (RAM); you cannot actually go wrong in the RAM department. RAM is your computer's short term memory. The more your RAM, the faster your computer will run. So buy a lot of RAM. This way, you will be sorted regardless of your recording style. It is therefore recommended that you get at least an eight gigabyte (8GB) RAM if you want your digital software to perform well.

A mantra you should always have at the back of your mind is that you can never have a too fast processor and too much RAM, no matter the computer brand. It is rather a question of your budget.

• Hard Drives; the hard drive is your computer's long term memory. Your hard drive plays two roles; the software role and the audio role. For your software hard drive, that is, to run your software effectively, the internal hard drive that comes with your computer is ideal. But, for your audio recording activities, you will need another hard drive that is capable of handling the pressure of storing and transferring audio data. This is because audio data eats up a lot of space. You should also have an additional external drive. This makes it 3 hard drives in total. The reason is, so you have a backup in case of any eventualities. As computer gurus say, if you have not duplicated your data in two separate locations, it does not exist. This luxury (yes, I call it a luxury), of course, only applies if you have the money.

There are two major types of hard drives; the solid-state drive (SSD for short) and the hard disk drive (HDD for short). The SSD is the ideal choice because when it comes to audio recording work, speed is what matters the most even more than space. Although SSD type hard drives are expensive and do not promise a lot of space, they are the fastest as they use flash memory. It is therefore recommended that you opt for an SSD hard drive, but if it puts too much strain on your budget, you can go for the HDD type, which is mechanical and cheaper but one with the spindle speed of 7200 RPM. It will also get the work done, especially if there is a tendency of you producing songs with at least 30 tracks and more.

The other parameters of a good hard drive you need to be on the lookout for apart from the spindle speed are; seek time and buffer size. Seek time is the time it takes to find the file stored on the hard drive. A seek time of not less than 10 milliseconds is recommended. The buffer size, also known as the cache buffer, is crucial in a hard drive as it stores data simultaneously as it is being transferred. A buffer of at least 8MB (8 megabytes) is recommended, although the manual from most hard drive manufacturers says size 2MB is ideal.

For music recording beginners with a somewhat tight budget, a 1TB (1 terabyte) drive with a 7200 3Gg/s RPM spindle speed, a 10 ms seek time, and a 32 MB buffer is ideal for you.

Sound Monitors

As opposed to using a simple stereo speaker that simply enhances/slake the sound of your recording, a studio monitor lets you hear exactly what is right or wrong with the sound you are making so you can make better sounds that sound naturally good on all speakers. The fact that you are a beginner and have a small studio space at home is more reason why you should buy the one with absolutely relevant specs.

Active speakers; there are 2 types of speakers based on the location of the amplifier; Active and Passive speakers. Active speakers have inbuilt amplifiers making the speaker a single package such that you just need to plug it into your plug power-point and your audio interface. This is why it is preferable passive speakers that function with a separate/external amplifier making it a 2 package speaker. This indicates that it takes more room than the Active speakers making it unsuitable for a small home studio space.

Frequency; it is recommended you get speakers that stretch to at least 40HZ or below, so you can hear exactly what your recordings sound like. There is no need for you to worry about the sounds being bland or deadpan because quite a number of studio monitors have a fairly muffled frequency response. It can be tweaked and manipulated until the desired result is realized. That is what software like Sonarworks Reference 3 is for.

Connectivity; It is better to avoid having to buy additional cables or wires to connect your speaker to your interface. Make sure the 2 equipment have compatible connectors.

That is, if your audio interface has an XLR or an RCA or a TRS connector, then your studio monitor should have the same.

Now that you know what to buy, it is important to know how to place the monitors in your studio so that you can get the best from it. Here are some pointers to help you;

In order to prevent sound dismemberment (funny, right?). Anything that doesn't make the sound come out right, that is, making it sound too loud or too amplified or with unsuitable frequency response, is the dismemberment of the sound and placing the monitor on a desk, either wooden or metallic actually dismembers the sound. For this reason, place the monitors on Auralex MoPads, which costs $30 to $40 before placing them on the desk.

You cannot place your studio monitors right beside each other. They must be at a well-calculated distance from each other. This is important, so there is a balance between the sounds coming out from each monitor hence, preventing any kind of sound lopsidedness. The distance between your monitors must also be equal to the distance between them and your ears.

Finally, based on all the recommended specs while taking into consideration your budget, the best you can do is a KRK Rokits 6G3, which costs about $370.

Headphones

Headphones are essential in a home recording studio. They are used for a lot of studio activities. They can be used in place of a studio monitor most of the time. Yes, the keyword is "most." Although they can well be used for mixing, a studio monitor is much better. The reason is that it is always better to mix in a room so you can measure the rate at which surrounding noise affects the sound as it is produced, then you will be able to adjust accordingly. Headphones make the sounds too perfect and flawless more than they actually are. Notwithstanding, headphones are ideal for a beginner. You can always upgrade to a studio monitor as you grow. You can then use the two interchangeably in areas they are the best option for optimum results. Moreover, you cannot purchase just any headphones. It has to be the ideal one with the following attributes;

Open-back or closed-back headphones; the two types of headphones are useful in the studio, although they both have their strengths and weaknesses. From its name, the two cups of the open-back have orifices through which sound passes easily. This characteristic makes them preferable for mixing as they produce quality sound thus, their strength and not ideal for recordings as they allow sounds to sip out, which is picked up by the microphone hence, their weakness.

Closed-back headphones, on the other hand, are ideal for recordings as they allow sound isolation hence their strength. The consequence of this is a deficiency in sound quality hence, their weakness.

Comfortability; headphones that allow for comfort is most recommended since you will be wearing them for hours on end. Therefore, they should have very soft foam padding and cups big enough to encompass the ears and not rest on it.

There are only 2recommended choices based on the parameters stated, really. First is the Sony MDR7506, which costs between $70 and $80. Second although a bit more expensive, is the Sennheiser HD 280, which costs $99.

Digital Audio Workstation (DAW) Software

This is the ultimate weapon and the backbone of any recording studio in recent times. Gone are the days of analog work stations, before the days of computers, whereby music producers have to work with a plethora of other studio props like MIDI sequencers, samplers, tape machines, etc. to produce great masterpieces. Now that producers can rely on DAW, which is a total package, studio life has become easier and faster even. The DAW is the powerhouse of your recording studio as it is, used for recording tracks, manipulating recorded tracks in your computer, mixing and mastering tracks, etc. it doesn't end here. It will be more expatiated in the next chapter.

Microphones (Mics)

To some extent, a music/audio studio looks lacking and incomplete without a microphone, and that is the fact. For a beginner, one microphone is enough, but as your recording operations increase, you can buy more. Microphones are essential as they are used to record vocals and instruments. Therefore, if you are a musician but a rookie producer, a microphone is a must-have, and not just any microphone but the ideal one. Here are some pointers;

Large-diaphragm Mics; Mics with Large-diaphragm do not only pick up sounds/vocals, but they also pick up on the emotions of the vocalist, thereby giving the sound additional authenticity. This is also attributed to the fact that they have a great frequency response.

Condenser Mics; Mics with a condenser pick up on the exact timbre or tone of the vocals or the instrument. This is due to the fact that the condenser is capable of picking high-frequency sounds, and expressing it so that it doesn't sound harsh. In short, it is a high pitch regulator.

Cardioids Mics; the sound which a cardioid Mic is designed to pick up is restricted to only sounds directly in front of it. This is actually a good attribute, especially for a beginner. A cardioid Mic helps you make certain only the sounds you want are recorded. Make sure your mouth or the mouth of your vocalist is very close to the front of the Mic while the back of it is turned towards the unwanted sounds.

The Audio-Technica AT2020 is budget-friendly as it costs less than $100, and it also has the above-listed attributes. Hence, it is highly recommended.

An additional advantage of a Large Diaphragm, Cardioid Condenser Mic is that it works well for both vocal sounds and instrumental sounds, unlike some other Mics that have compatibility with just one type of sound. They are also cheap (surprising, right?).

There is one important fact to note. Yes, USB Mics are cheaper even more than large-diaphragm Mics, more in vogue, and do not need an interface to connect to the computer, but you have to try as much as possible to avoid them because they are not as durable as the traditional microphones.

Audio Interface/Sound Card

Modern computers these days have an in-built sound card. This means you can make recordings with your laptop, desktop, or Ipad. But for serious music production, you need an audio interface. An audio interface is a medium that connects all your input devices; Mics, studio monitors, MIDI keyboard, headphones, etc. to your computer so that you can make great vocal and instrumental recordings and then edit those recordings on your DAW software to get the best result. An audio interface converts all the signals from your Mics, headphones, and studio monitor into the computer language so it can be interpreted and utilized for recording, mixing, and mastering. As a home recording studio owner and a rookie at that, what you require is an "all in one" modern digital audio interface that will be compact and will not take space. The all in one characteristic of the interface indicates that it has; microphone pre-amps, headphone amps, digital conversion, monitor management, and DI boxes built-in so that you do not have to purchase them as stand-alone equipment. It is also budget-friendly.

There are 3 types of ports through which the interface is connected to the computer; USB, Thunderbolt, FireWire, and PCI. The PCI has the advantage of transfer speed over the other types of interface, although it is old and rarely used now compared to the other two interface types. The audio interface you choose must be compatible with your computer such that it has the same port as your computer. Furthermore, be certain that your interface has the right type and quantity input ports to plug your microphone and/or musical instrument and the right output port to plug your studio monitors either, RCA, XLR, 1/4", or 1/8".

Based on budget-friendliness, quality, and the requirement stated, the recommended audio interface is the Focusrite Scarlett 2i2 USB Audio interface, which costs about $160.

Optional Studio Props

The following studio units are termed optional only for you as a beginner since you are just starting and still finding your footing in the music recording community. By the time you grow and expand from home or bedside or portable studio to a more standard and professional studio, you will have to get them.

MIDI keyboard; this comes in handy if you are interested in playing musical instruments, and you do not have the physical instruments. The MIDI keyboard takes the role of virtual instruments allowing you to play any and every kind of instrument. The need for a MIDI keyboard is not pressing for a beginner in record making. You can still make do with the virtual instrument in your computer software. If you are going to venture into professional beat making and electronic music production, then it is a very necessary tool and not optional.

Speaker stands; it has already been established in the speaker section that the speakers can be placed on a desk, just not directly on the desk. Your budget and deficiency in studio space will not allow it.

Cables; if you try as much as possible to follow the directives stated in the earlier sections about connectivity, you would not need to make additional expenses buying cables.

Mic stands; this is what holds your microphone up in the studio. It is actually useful in a home studio, but it is a studio unit you can do without if your budget cannot carry it

Pop filter; pop filters are like nets that are designed to catch air blasts when you talk into the Mic. These air blasts do not help your sounds but rather dismembers it. Rather than buying a pop filter for your Mic, you just have to be ready to make some adjustments on your DAW to extricate any effect the air blasts might have had on your recordings.

These so-called optional studio units are not so optional in a pro record studio because no matter if there are alternatives, albeit convincing, they are quite essential in making music that is a masterpiece and promises to be a hit.

Chapter Two: Beginner Software for 2020

It is important you are not misinformed that only software workstations exist. When you go into the studio rooms of the big record labels, you will see a real longboard with a lot of controls, buttons, input and output ports, which sometimes encompasses the whole length or breadth of the studio. That longboard is an analog console made up of a hardware workstation. It allows for a lot of hands-on recording, editing, and mixing. The days of analog music production are long gone; we are now in the digital era. Music producers either, beginner, intermediate, professional, or even the bigwigs in the industry who have the money to acquire all the studio equipment has keyed into the modern way of doing things (software!). It is important to evolve as technology is evolving, so you do not end up being left behind.

Technology has made music production somewhat easier through the Digital Audio Workstation. The computer-based DAW comprises the hardware and software components. It allows for compact music production. The hardware components of a DAW comprise of; your computer, audio interface, microphones, or any other input devices and, of course, the software component, which is made up of what we know as DAW. This denotes that there is no music producer worth his salt that does not use a DAW system. Apart from the software component of the DAW system, the hardware components have been discussed extensively in the previous sections. Both components work hand in hand to record, edit, mix, and playback tracks.

The DAW software application is installed on your computer and operated through it to make tracks. The software has been designed in such a way that you can do all that is necessary to make an entire song on your computer only, through the DAW system. The relevance of software-based DAW cannot be underestimated. It is to a musician what the engine is to a car, what lead is to a pencil, and so on (you get what I am hinting right?).

As a beginner, choosing the right DAW for you will be the most difficult step you take in your music production journey because your DAW software in the brain box of your whole studio set. To pick the ideal DAW for you is more like flirting. You have to be willing to try out the demos of a lot of different software to know the one that is best for you as an individual music producer. Have it at the back of your mind that all the available types of DAW software are not bad and will get the job done based on their individual strengths. Here are some pointers to help you make an informed and calculated decision that will benefit you in both the short-run and the long-run;

The entirety of your computer system should inform your decision because there must be 100 percent compatibility between your DAW software choice and your computer. Some software is only compatible with Macs, some are only compatible with Windows PC, while others are compatible with both. Therefore, to be on the safer side, it is more beneficial to choose the one that works across the board in the event of collaborations with other music producers or in the event you change computer systems. This way, you will still be able to use the software you are already familiar with.

• Compatibility with audio plug-ins is also a crucial factor that should inform your DAW software decision. Plug-ins are either incorporated into DAW as an auxiliary program from the manufacturers or are external units that can be amalgamated to it. Plug-ins are used majorly for Equalization, Compression, and Reverb of tracks. These three processes are just enough to model, manipulate, and blend all recorded sounds; vocals, instruments, etc. into your desired result. Plug-ins are the major tools used in the audio engineering aspect of music production. They will be discussed more extensively further in the book.

• The music production objectives you seek to achieve should also inform your software choice. This is essential because some DAWs are stronger in some aspects of music production than in some others. For instance, the type of DAWs used by a music producer leaning more towards electronic music or beat making will likely be quite different from the type a music producer leaning towards arrangement and music sheet printing will use. This is attributed to the fact that not all DAWs are forged alike. Some have faster workflows than others, others run with specific types of plug-ins while others run with some other types, and you get the gist. This, in fact, is majorly why it is recommended to try out demos of various types of DAW, so you know what you are buying before you actually buy it.

• As far as choice parameters go, affordability, and yes! I mean money is at the top. Try as much as possible to buy what is just enough for you to achieve your objective. The reason for this stems from the fact that you might end up buying a DAW with more features than you need and will end up using.

What Software Should You Use?

The sheer number of music software in the market these days has provided a lot of options to choose from. Your eventual choice after some trials should be what you, your computer, your music production goals, and your budget prefer and most comfortable with. Based on market reviews performed in the later arm of 2019, in preparation for the year 2020, here are some options for you, especially those most ideal for beginners and compatible with both Macintosh and Windows computer systems.

Image-Line FL Studio 20 Producer Edition

This edition out of 4 editions is most ideal for a beginner who is on a budget. It costs about $200 to $250 online.

● FL Studio comes with a free trial package with an unlimited time limit. Therefore, you can practice and practice to your heart contents.

● It has the capacity to handle a plethora of tracks without or with a very exiguous amount of hitch. You can also work with as many inputs as you like and in a go.

● FL Studio is the definition of a total package as it is capable of performing all the necessary stages of making a complete song, and excellently well too. From the desire to make a record/track/song to its actualization and even audio post-production (involves merging tracks produced with videos, television, etc.).

● The FL Studio is one of a kind. It helps you achieve fits in music production that have been deemed impossible or too difficult. Furthermore, it's editing, mixing, and mastery capabilities are very extensive such that no matter the rhythm, pitch, harmony, beat, volume, timbre, and so on, the level you desire FL Studio makes it a done deal.

- It also comes with synthesizers that will enable you to produce any sound you fancy; piano, harp, electric guitar, all kinds of drums, and many more.

- Once you buy the FL Studio software, you do not have to pay for updates throughout the time it is in use. You do not also need to buy plug-ins as the software has more than enough incorporated in it, and if you have to for one reason or the other, it pairs with it magnificently well.

- The software is helping to produce music, and at the same time, it trains you on how to do it.

Ableton Live 10 Suite Multitrack Recording Software

Unlike other DAW software, Ableton Live is the most compatible with live performances. This indicates that record, track or song manipulations can be done while it is being played back after mixing. This characteristic is peculiar to Ableton's live 10.

- Ableton Live makes music production seem like solving a jigsaw puzzle. Different kinds of sounds are deconstructed and reconstructed until a perfect fit is achieved.

- Ableton live 10 is ideal for DJs, concert performances, clubs, and the likes because of its peculiar attribute. It is both a producer and performer software.

- Ableton live 10 Achilles' heel is the fact that all sounds produce whether vocals or instrumental can be converted to act like MIDI, hence, the flexibility attribute it gives tracks, already recorded and/or on-the-fly tracks.

- It takes a lot of time to master the features of the Ableton live, but once you do, music production will then seem like a child's play.

- Ableton live 10 also comes with a free trial package. So try and try and try till you become more dexterous with it.

- One set back to our goal of budget-friendly DAWs is that Ableton Live is on the expensive side. It costs about $500 to $600 online.

Reaper, The Beginner Version

This software is way easier to learn compared to FL Studio and even Ableton Live.

- Like the FL Studio, Reaper is ideal for music producers with leanings towards arrangement, music scriptwriting, downloading script, and music sheet printing.

- Just like the two software already mentioned, Reaper allows for all manners of high quality/professional sound recording, editing, mixing, sound manipulation, and so on.

- Reaper is so cheap that the fact that it doesn't have a sound library can be overlooked. It costs about $60 to $70 online. See how cheap it is.

- Reaper's lack of a sound library is redeemed by the fact that it has a plethora of plug-in effects including equalization effect, compression effect and reverb among others which are the core ones, and the ability to pair with external sounds stored either on external hard drives, third-party plug-ins or online data storage facilities.

• Reaper also allows for easy export of sound finished products to different mediums in different data forms such as mp3, wave, AIFF, etc. as it does for the import and amalgamation of various music data from various music directories. It is a very flexible software indeed.

• Reaper, unlike FL Studio and Ableton Live, has just one version and does not mean it is inferior; in fact, it is either at par with them or almost at par.

PreSonus Studio One 4 Prime

PreSonus is one of the easiest DAW software to operate.

• The strong suit of this software is its fast and easy mixing and mastering abilities. Presonus allows you to drag and drop instruments easily, sample beats, plug-in effects, and even third party sounds to the arrange window where they will be merged, tweaked, edited, compiled to form layers of audio to form one single, final and beautiful track. On Presonus, mixing is akin to solving a puzzle, fun, right! PreSonus makes music production fun.

• I am not certain if the fact that it is continually packed with new updates is a blessing or a curse. It is up to you to decide what it is for you. You might be the type that is slow to adapt to change. In this situation, a constant update that is synonymous with constant change might feel like a curse to you. On the other hand, if you are a person who gladly welcomes change, then Presonus' constant updates are a blessing to you.

• PreSonus Studio One 4 Prime costs about $300 to $350 online.

• Presonus also has quite a number of plug-in effects and virtual instruments which function as well as MIDI. The software runs not only really fast but really well too.

Avid Pro Tools

Overtime, Avid pro tools software has been the most generally known music production software in pro, intermediate, and even the beginner circles. Quite a number of seasoned music produce and upcoming music producers believe that without proficiency in pro tools, even if you are proficient in any of the other prominent software, you are not a professional enough music producer. This is how powerful Avid pro tools software is.

• Avid Pro Tools is the ideal DAW software to teach and to learn music production.

• Avid Pro Tools is one of the best for mixing and mastering why? It is equipped with over 60 virtual instruments and a highly equipped sound library that provides you with varieties of sound samples so that you have a lot of editing and tweaking options.

• It is also equipped with an application that allows you to run the software with wireless internet access.

• Avid Pro tools also come with utility plug-ins, which gives you an even bigger playfield. Utility plug-ins are additional plug-ins that come in handy when you need to expand your playing field. For instance, utility plug-in help to boost signals from external plug-ins or music data from external drives.

• The whole music production shindig is performed excellently well on the software, composing, arranging, recording, sound processing, especially mixing and mastering.

- Apart from music production processes, pro tools also work excellently well for pro-production processes. Therefore, it is the most used software in the movie and showbiz industries.

- Despite the fact that it is on the expensive side at the cost of $600 to $700, it is very popular and generally preferred. There must be something the software is doing right compared to its competition.

Apple Logic Pro X

Logic is very well created DAW with all the best attributes of the other software and very exiguous amount of their flaws. Unfortunately, it is only compatible with Macintosh computers. Its level of advancement and sophistication is on the same level as Avid pro tools, if not higher. Frankly speaking, Logic is not the software for beginners. It is rather for professional/seasoned producers who have been long in the game. It is not recommended to start using this particular software as a beginner. Get used to music production with packages that come with trials, then when you become more confident in your abilities and, of course, have more money saved up, you can get a Logic pro x for yourself and make a place for yourself in the professional league. Let us run the numbers; Apple Logic Pro x costs $200 to $250 online.

Free DAW

As a beginner, it is key that you start your music production journey with free DAW software. The free software provides you with a platform to learn on the job as the case may be. It also provides you with the opportunity to test all kinds of software until you decide the one that is a perfect fit. Frankly speaking, free software is majorly for practice, for you to learn the trade because it is packed with lots of limitations and setbacks. At the end of the day, it is very necessary you convert to paid DAW so you can produce much better sounds that will sell. Here are some of the cons associated with free DAW:

• Most free DAW software comes with very few plug-ins and does not allow third-party plug-ins. Furthermore, they are also deficient in plug-in effects. At the least, you need the three core plug-in effects (equalizer, compressor, and reverb) to be able to achieve audio editing/mixing to some extent.

• The virtual instruments that come with the free DAW are quite basic such that you cannot really do much in the mixing department to an above-average level.

• In general, free software does not make available all the features, characteristics that allow you to strive as a professional music producer.

• Free DAW software requires a very stable internet with high transmission capacity. Although there is some free music software that can be operated offline.

Let us discuss a few of the best available free DAW software/audio editors:

❖ Pro Tools First, pro tools, the paid version, is majorly for professional music production. Pro Tools First is the free model of pro tools, which is especially for beginners. It comes with 16 virtual instruments and a fairly equipped sound samples library containing beats, loops, drums, etc. for audio editing. Pro tools first come with 23 utility plug-in effects which enable it to accommodate 4 inputs at a time.

❖ Rosegarden; did not originally accommodate audio recording when it was first created. Now, it allows audio recording and even editing minimally since it is majorly just a MIDI sequencer. Just like the majority of the free DAWs, Rosegarden accommodates only and specifically 5 Linux plug-ins per record. This might seem too exiguous,' but it is quite ideal for a beginner, music student, rookie composer, and the likes because it is very easy to learn and master.

❖ Reaper; Reaper is globally acknowledged as one of the best DAW software for beginners. Reaper is not free technically; rather, it has unlimited trials. You can test this fact by setting the date on your computer to 2040. You will discover that Reaper still works. This software, even the trials, is top-notch in recording, editing. It doesn't discriminate with track types, whether MIDI, video, or audio. It accommodates them all. See the previous session for more on the attributes of Reaper.

❖ PreSonus; Presonus, unlike Reaper, does not come with unlimited trials but comes with a 30-day trial within which you can learn how to mix and master sounds. One beautiful attribute of PreSonus is that it has little to no restrictions. It doesn't restrict any type of plug-ins or any genre of music. See the previous session for more on the attributes of Reaper.

❖ Bandlab; Bandlab works only with a stable internet connection and only on chrome. Bandlab is very easy to understand and operate. Bandlab allows you to easily drag and drop instruments, sample beats, plug-in effects on the timeline. Bandlab is one of that simple and basic music software that runs on mobile phones as well as tabs/laptops/desktops. It allows you to save your work no matter how many they are. Bandlab is strictly beginner software because of its limitations, which make it not ideal for professional music production.

The software listed above may be free and easier to handle than the likes of FL studio; however, you still need to take some time to practice to get the hang of it.

In all the sessions so far, plug-ins, virtual instruments have been mentioned quite often, but do you know what they really are and how they work or are used?

What is an Audio Plug-In?

A plug-in is software within the software or external software merged with a computer program. A plug-in enhances the functionalities of the software/program it inhabits or is merged to. Audio plug-in amplifies the musical performance of a computer program such as DAW, which majorly comprises of effect units (EQ, reverb, delay ...) for signal processing and sound synthesizers and samplers. There are three classifications of Audio plug-ins. These classifications are based on the functions of audio plug-ins in a DAW program.

• Audio plug-ins modify extant sound samples

- Audio plug-ins create sound samples with sound synthesizers

- Audio plug-ins analyses extant sound samples.

Audio plug-ins on DAW software (plug-in host) is synonymous with applications on your mobile phone. Different applications perform different functions on the phone, as you well know. There are those that help to maintain the integrity of the phone; there are those for fun (games), there are those for creating data (camera, Microsoft office), those for communication, for storage, etc. Some come with the phone from the manufacturer while you have to download others. These scenarios also apply for music software and plug-ins.

Audio plug-ins interact with any platform through an interface. These interactions are in three categories;

- Interaction with the computer and other electronic devices: the interaction between an audio plug-in and a computer is mediated by the GUI (Graphical User Interface). The GUI uses graphical icons, just like the application icons in mobile phones. When you click on such icons, it takes you straight to the plug-in timeline or arrange-window. The host here is the computer, which creates these icons based on information from the manufacturer or from the plug-in.

- Interaction with a host plug-in, which may be another plug-in or software that runs the plug-in: For this instant, the software in question is DAW software, for example, Reaper, Pro Tools, etc. software): this interaction is mediated by the API (Application Programming Interface). The API dictates the program instruction, the organization, management, and data storage style that are incorporated in the plug-in so that it can be loaded by the host plug-in. Furthermore, the manner through which the audio plug-in responds to an instruction from DAW and how DAW responds is also specified by the API.

In simple terms, plug-ins talk to their host computers through the GUI and to their host software or application through the API.

What are audio signal processing, audio synthesis, and audio effects?

These three procedures are the most crucial aspects of any audio plug-in. They are the major catalysts of the DAW software boost and enhancement a plug-in establishes.

• Audio signal processing is the computerized manipulation of audio impulses/signals. Audio impulses are the computerized representation of sound waves, which may be either in digital or analog forms. The focus will be on the digital because the music production has since evolved and still evolving past the analog age for a long time now and because digital anything promises more efficiency than analog.

• Audio synthesis is the computerized imitation or creation of audio impulses through a musical instrument called an audio synthesizer.

• An audio effect is the alteration of audio impulses. It involves changing how an audio signal sounds.

Simply put; Audio signal processing ≡ Audio synthesis + Audio effects + Audio broadcasting.

Forms of audio plug-ins and their compatibility with DAWs and computer systems.

There are quite a lot of plug-in formats; however, we will be focusing majorly on those that are compatible with Windows and Macintosh computer systems.

- Virtual Studio Technology (VST): VST plug-ins come as either virtual studio instruments (VSTi) or virtual studio effects (VSTfx). VST plug-in format is responsible for integrating audio synthesis and audio effects in DAWs.

VST instruments (some popular ones are; Nexus, Gladiator, Discovery, FM8, Reakto, etc.) typically are either Virtual Synthesizers or Virtual samplers. Several recreate the design and sound of renowned hardware synthesizers. Then, VST effects (audio effects e.g., reverb, phasers) processes the created digital audio. VST is available for Macintosh, Windows, and Linux computers. It was developed by Steinberg. The host plug-ins that run the VST plug-in format are Ableton Live, Reaper, FL studio, and Logic pro among others.

- Audio units (AU): AU is compatible with only Apple's Macintosh computer systems. It was developed by Apple. It comes with the operating system, which therefore means that its GUI and API are informed by the system. They are similar to VST such that, they also create and process (audio pitch correction, time stretching and vocal processing) and audio impulses but with marginal latency in near-real-time. AU runs in Apple DAW software such as Logic Pro, Logic pro x, Garageband, and as a third-party plug-in in Mac DAW software such as Ableton Live, Reaper, and Studio one among others.

- Avid Audio Extention (AAX): this plug-in format was published when Avid made the 64-bit Pro tools. This indicates that it was custom made by Avid Technology for Avid Pro tools software since a 64-bit plug-in was needed. AAX also transforms and synthesizes audio samples. It is available on Windows and Mac.

• Real-time Audio Suite (RTAS): This particular plug-in format is vastly limited as it only runs in one to ten versions of Pro Tools. This is attributed to the fact that it was developed by Digidesign now Avid Technology. Unlike the digital signal processing cards used in Pro tools systems, RTAS taps into the processing capabilities of its host computer to process audio signals.

• TDM (Time-division Multiplexing): A version of Pro Tools plug-ins that square measure put in on outboard hardware like dedicated digital signal Processors for ultra-high temerity and quality. TDM Plug-ins are typically put in high-quality studio setups equipped with dedicated chips that analyze the audio signal instead of making the computer's processor do the processing.

• Standalone: Some developers additionally supply a standalone version of their products. Because the name suggests, this cannot be truly a plug-in. It is simply a version of the audio plug-in that will be launched, such as you would a traditional desktop application. It doesn't need a Corrine bird to figure. This can be a convenient approach for users to use the plug-in and is usually useful for live performances.

Types Of Plug-Ins

When it involves the various sorts of plug-ins, there are virtually too many to count. With numerous choices to decide from, they will be classified based on their use in the recording studio. And if you are inclined towards buying one cluster of plug-ins rather than choosing and selecting from the following list, you will find quality choices with the Complete Avid Plug-in package, Apogee FX package, and McDSP Pack Bundle.

• Equalizer (EQ): EQ is a processor that permits you to spice up and cut targeted bands of frequencies within the sound range. Equalizers are commonly used to enliven tracks that sound dry and boosting low frequencies to make a track/song more powerful and more promising to be a hit!

As a beginner, you most likely do not have the funds to buy supplementary studio props (acoustic and bass panels), which mind you are quite necessary in order to make great sounds. This is where equalizers come in. They take the role of the acoustic and bass panels by adjusting the sound frequencies and range in the studio until it is balanced, and you hear what you want to.

• Compressor Audio Plug-ins: Compressors are simply the foremost usually rivaled hardware devices. There are tons of choices to select from; it occasionally appears overwhelming. The great news is that each mechanical device has one thing distinctive to supply, which will assist you in improving your record. While equalizers alter the frequency response or tone of an audio impulse, compressors alter the amount or dynamic response given by an audio impulse. Compressors are popularly used to manage the forces at work during a performance. To explain this in simple terms, compressors reduce the intensity of loud sounds by making them quieter and intensify quiet sounds by making them louder. With an exiguous amount of practice, compressors may be employed to intensify the brief or slight sound, such as the hit of a drum. They prevent the clipping of bass notes and inflicting distortion. Compressors can be used to fashion the quality of sound to your taste or a different type.

- Delay/Reverb Audio plug-in: In the early analog days of recording, the sole option to give more reverb to a sound was to maneuver the Mic, so it is positioned at a considerable distance from the source of the sound. This method has, however, been abandoned since EMT discharged the EMT one hundred and forty- reverb plate in 1957, along with an assortment of other tools for emulating the studio space in audio mixing.

Added to the spring and plate design that appear analog, reverb plug-ins additionally provided a collection of systems to imitate how spaces such as churches, event halls, chambers, etc. sound like. The Reverb compatible plug-ins are often applied to imitate peculiar spaces such as huge repositories and little canisters.

Delay plug-ins work somewhat alike. Some are imitations of tape delays that are antique, whereas the others inaugurate all-new computer programs that might solely be attained by a system to produce sounds and effects.

- Sound cadence/Vocal refining Audio Plug-ins: Sound cadence/Vocal Plug-ins are potentially the foremost powerful tool among the audio plug-in collection. The sound cadence refining software package permits you to adjust the scale of any and every note in a rendition. These software packages also work on simply vocals, too; several engineers make use of sound cadence correction plug-ins also to tweak/harmonize recordings made from instruments.

Getting the proper vocals is far more than simply singing the correct note, for this reason, an assortment of vocal process gears to harmonize your sound recording routine is also quite necessary, together with professional comping, de-esers for clearing the sizzle/wheezing-like sounds, and other available vocal suites, that are filled with potent audio effects for radio-primed vocals.

• Noise Reduction Plug-ins (Audio): Noise reduction plug-ins do precisely what you'd expect; they scale back unwelcome noise in records to enhance the quality of the sound. These plug-ins do not have an analog simulation; they're all digital. It involves the use of advanced algorithms to observe and repair issues in audio recordings.

Many completely different forms of noise reduction plug-ins exist, every with a specialized task like removing plosives, removing buzz, or removing clicks. Most of those plug-ins are packed in a cluster, therefore, making it easy for you to take on any downside that you come across.

• Amp/Speaker Modeling Audio Plug-ins: Plug-ins have gotten really smart in modeling analog instrumentation that they've extended past the conventional signaling processors into modeling whole guitar rigs. Right from the kind of tubes within the head, the cab drivers, to the Mic choice and placement, speaker modeling plug-ins, and stringed instrument amp allow for easier capturing of professional-sounding stringed instrument tones without grievances because of noise. Recreate the precise rigs of some famous guitarists by making use of genuine imitations of amps created by Fender, Marshall, Vox, and many more.

• Microphone Preamp Audio Plug-ins: Microphone preamp plug-ins are custom built to recreate vintage, analog console sound from Neve, API, SSL, and lance, coupled with standalone model styles from corporations like Telefunken. Apart from modeling the preamp sound, several plug-ins conjointly recreate the sound of the whole circuit for a very authentic tone. It is routine for preamp plug-ins to incorporate controls to process filters, phase, and stereo. Furthermore, EQ is included in models such as the Neve 1073, Trident A-range, and SSL E-Series.

- Microphone Modeling Audio Plug-ins: The latest improvement in audio simulation technology has opened up an entirely new world of prospects for engineers and producers. With one Mic, you'll be able to reproduce sounds of vintage microphones from Neumann, to Telefunken, RCA, and many more sounds that can fill a medium-size locker completely.

Rather than committing to one sound till you're able to lay aside enough cash to create an accomplished Mic suite, systems of microphone modeling allow you to experiment with loads of samples as long as you are able to click a button on your keyboard or mouse. You'll be able even to modify the model of the microphone as harmosoon as you finish recording, providing you the ability to record immediately you are inspired and subsequently perfect your chain signal.

It is quite important you know that no one can completely assure you that one particular software, or plug-in, or any other music apparatus is the best. What is best is you try as much as possible to amass knowledge by trying out the demos, trials, and the free stuff, practice with them, become an authority in a few of the available options, the ones you deem best as per your preference. The book has tried as much as possible to provide viable options. It is now left to acclimatize your personal preference.

Chapter Three: Getting Started in 2020

In the earlier session of the book, it was mentioned that you do not need to go to a glorified college or specialized music school to be able to produce music. With the rate at which technology and music technology, in particular, is evolving and growth of the number of technology-savvy individuals in the world today, this claim is not baseless. However, you still need to know the fundamentals/basics of music in general. The elements/rudiments of music, the consistently reoccurring terminologies you will definitely always come across, and so on.

A crucial part of the rudiments of music is music theory. Most musicians already know the fundamentals of music theory. In fact, musicians put music theory into practice all the time. They just might not know the terminologies/technicalities of the concept they already know and already put to practice.

Meaning Of Music Theory

Music theory is the language musicians adopt to explain and describe the phenomena discerned in a musical composition. Music theory defines the core aspects of music and provides a system for musicians to speak their postulations to 1 another.

The ideas and rules that structure music theory are a lot like the grammatical rules that govern written communication (which additionally developed once individuals had with success discovered the mechanism of speaking with each other). Whilst having the ability to transcribe language induced its attainability for individuals far from each other to "hear" conversations and stories the exact method the author wanted, having the ability to transcribe music permits, musicians, to study and play compositions precisely the way the composer predetermined.

As a Music Producer, Must I Know Music Theory?

Music theory could appear akin to a stuffy educational endeavor that turns to create music into a chore. This is so not true. Learning one aspect or more of music theory will serve as an added advantage to all musicians. Understanding music theory ideas is the key to progressing on your instrument, improved songwriting, and breaking through artistic blocks.

You can obtain the vital elements of music theory by learning on your own and applying the ideas to your everyday music production exercise.

Music Theory Proper

If you want to learn anything, it is best you start from the foundation, the basics. This will not be an exception. There are three core building blocks that make up every musical composition, regardless of style, genre, etc. These foundations are;

Melody: Melody is a linear sequence of notes you hear as one entity. The melody of a song is the lead to the backing components and could be a combination of pitch and rhythm. Sequences of notes that comprise melody are musically gratifying and are usually the matchless part of a song.

From catchy choruses to infectious stringed instrument riffs, melodies outline the music you recognize and love as a result of the fact that they are the aspects of a song you might possibly recollect. Therefore melodies are essential aspects of all types of music.

Harmony: One of the essential elements of a song is its harmony. However, it might just be arduous to effect right. It is not a must you understand every little factor regarding music to be artistic. However, there are some elements of music that are considered necessary to unlock your inbuilt songwriting talent, and harmony is at the top of the list. It doesn't matter if you are a seasoned music producer or a beginner, learning the theory of music has huge creative advantages.

Harmony is achieved when two (or more) separate pitch notes are engaged at once. The strategic combination of the distinct pitches within a chord alongside the overall structure of a song chord may be referred to as harmony. However, in music theory, the basic concept of harmony typically refers to chord composition, chord progressions, and chord qualities. The term Harmony is only applied when the instruments in question are pitched; therefore, clapping your hands and clumping your feet at once won't produce harmony.

Harmony may also be associated with vocals, but it is generally generated due to the combination of multi-pitched instruments like guitars, pianos, and synths—or a combination of single-pitched instruments creating completely unique notes simultaneously, like 2 folks singing along.

Making music through captivating and genuine harmonies could be an important ability for a beginner who wants to create and produce music.

Rhythm: Rhythm is one of the elemental aspects of music theory. To create nice harmonies and melodies, you would like to know the way rhythm works and the way it's employed in your tracks.

Rhythm occurs when music is methodically divided into beats within a bar that is replayed at a specific time interval, speed, and tempo. It is the language spoken and understood between musicians and even among different songs.

Rhythm is an arduous phenomenon to define. It has contrasting meanings to different people. For instance, a group of drummers will tell you it is all about finding a drumbeat pattern; a band will tell you rhythm occurs when each member of the band, whether human or instrument, finds their groove and balance is struck.

As you can see, rhythm is a thing of perspective and cannot be chained to a specific status quo. You can create rhythmic beats on your DAW with your DAW swing.

The fundamentals have been briefly established; now, let us move on to the rudiments of music theory. The idea behind the musical movements that you see every day, no matter which instrument you play, is the basis of music theory. They are terminologies you already inculcate when you just sing or play one instrument or the other. These rudiments are also the building blocks for the fundamentals (melody, harmony, and rhythm). Here they are:

Music Notation/Notes; having a good idea of how the music language is written is the foundation for increasing your awareness of theory. Even if you're not playing or performing music from a recorded score, you can connect the dots between what you hear and what you play on a screen.

Music Keys; Keys are the harmonic and melodic background for a song's behavior; they provide a model that lets musicians know which notes to play with each other when performing. A series of sharps or flats (accidentals) called a key signature specifies the identity of a piece of music. At the beginning of a music row, a key signature clearly indicates which notes must be changed from their initial state to reflect the key. Before emerging, a song may begin in a certain key and finish in another, or visit some other key. This refers to a key change.

Music chords; when you have the groundwork of developing theoretical knowledge, you will immerse yourself in the fundamentals of musical study. The chords are separate units of harmony. They emerge once a band of consonant pitches sounds together. The interaction between the pitch of two frequencies is defined as the interval. The pattern of intervals within the chord influences the value of the chord.

The manner the pitches blend in the context of the chord, and the manner the individual chords communicate with each other determines the meaning of the track's peculiarity. Bringing chords together in series is among the most important aspects of songwriting. A musically satisfying series of chords is considered a progression of chords.

Music scale; Music scales are the raw material for melodies. Any melodic musical verse with a song tune depends on a scale for its form. A scale is a concurrent bundle of notes with a particular arrangement of tones and semitones. This arrangement informs the tone of the scale and the manner in which it is used in tracks.

Varying scales add varying moods, feelings, and attributes to a song, therefore, leading to the birth of varying melodic avenues.

There are a plethora of scale types out there, each one with a distinct melodic designation of its own. However, the two fundamental ones are; the major and the minor scales.

Scales and chords have almost identical effects when it gets down to creating a song's sonic peculiarity. Scales and chords are the basic tenets you ought to have knowledge about to begin producing good music.

We have just scratched the surface of the entirety of music theory. The emphasis made on the fundamentals is meant to give you an idea, however, if you would like to go deeper, there are a lot of online articles, videos, and classes that will give you what you need.

Making an acquaintance with the fundamentals is a good start for music production in 2020. What is now tenable and is likely to facilitate excellence is the readiness to arm oneself with all the necessary weapons that promise to give you an edge in your work and leisure communities.

Chapter Four: Current Trends and The Future Of Music

Music Production's Current Climate

Everything in the music scene seems to be in a fierce hurry somewhere. A particular trend or style of music does not last long on the shelf before it is thrown, and some other style or trend takes its place. This is the reality. This is the status quo. What you have to do so you are not left aimlessly floating is to ride the tide as it comes. Create a flexible/adaptable skin which you can shrug on when things do not go according to plan.

Due to the high-speed development of the music industry, it not only the music production scene that is evolving, the music sale and music consumption (music business) scene are also changing and not necessarily for the better.

The music business is going through a growth spurt. This can be attributed to the 10% rise in total income to $4.6 billion in 2018, with streaming taking about three-quarters of it. This has not really affected the market's strength even if it relies heavily on the proceeds from streaming. The "market" looks much the same in 2019 as it has for the past two decades, just a little difference majorly in the technology arena. Yes, proceeds from the sale of physical music are only a fraction of what they used to be because people do not really buy music in cassettes and CDs any more, which has led to the eradication of most stores that are mainly into the sale of records. However, we still have major record labels, Artistes and repertoires, launch dates, global tours, publishing deals, recording industry managers. You know the drill.

A decade from now, a lot of changes will occur. In fact, it has already begun. For instance, see what is going on in the car business now about self-driving cars that are being introduced into the market. A considerable amount of the steps involved in driving a car like; the driving lessons, the driving license, and the likes will become a distant memory. Let us see what the future scene is brimming to look like:

Physical Media in the Music Community is Dying

In recent years, people's sentimentality towards physical media (CDs, cassettes, and vinyl) has created extra income for the music industry. It is no news that the sound quality from CDs and cassettes has been perfectly replicated in streaming. However, that is not the case for vinyl. Streaming has not been able to replicate that unique tone that accompanies it (even Tidal is still struggling to achieve it). For this reason, vinyl has momentarily resumed as a solid business line for record labels.

Despite this positivity from the vinyl sale angle, players in the music industry should curb their enthusiasm, because unlike cross colors or producers of sports apparel, the sales in physical music are propelled by sentimental feelings towards ' 80s and' 90s. Nostalgic feelings would not last for long. This fact is evident as 75% of the revenue from the music industry was from streaming services in 2018. This percentage will continue to rise to leave an insignificant piece (as tiny as just 5% or less) for the physical media market.

The Upsurge of the Hip-Hop Artist Residency

Quite a number of musicians who have been long in the game will assure you they love everything about having shows, concerts, performances but do not like tours that take them abroad. Why? Boredom, the fact that they might not get good food to eat, living in hotels, you know the drill. Repetition of this cycle takes its toll, both mentally and physically. The good news is that steps are being taken in places like Los Angeles, Niagara Falls, New York and other places in the United States and abroad that are famous music concert destinations, in form of 5000 to 10,000 and above capacity pavilions/arenas being constructed so that musicians can have their crowded, noisy shows without having to leave their home base. Do not get it twisted. Musicians going for tours abroad cannot be completely eradicated, but it will be drastically reduced.

Record Labels are Going to Cease to Exist

Let us analyze this. What have record labels been doing, and are they still trying to do despite all the upcoming obstacles as a result of technological advancements and plain old change? Well, record labels majorly dabble in Artist & Repertoire (A&R), distribution, and marketing. The tradition of record labels going out on the streets to search for talent, then nurturing that talent till it becomes a worldwide sensation is becoming obsolete why? Social media followings, comments, likes, and dislikes dictates who the latest talent is. This has really rendered the A&R department of the record labels completely superseded.

For the marketing and distribution aspects, artists of today are self-reliant. They market themselves to their followers, who then market them to their own followers. It goes on and on like that till they go viral. On the distribution scene, artists simply sell their songs to those that provide streaming services and the likes at a reasonable fee. The things artists cannot easily get are the contacts, finances, experiences, and networks that record labels, especially the bigwigs (Warner, EMI, Sony, and Universal music groups) that have accumulated over the years. As a result, record labels will have the option of either switching to another business or taking advantage of the edge they have and becoming solely music advertisement firms (remember! ride the tide).

Hit Songs Will Last Longer on Music Charts

Now that streaming of music is the order of the day, the fact that a song was not a hit or was not at the top of the chart the moment it was released does not mean it would remain like that forever. Furthermore, the songs that hit the top of the charts at first release can also last longer at the top of the charts since the more the song is streamed, the more it is regarded as a hit.

Virtual reality is going to be a viable tool in the music industry

Just as some musicians do not like to travel for shows and music festivals, some Fans do not also fancy traveling long distances, which may be in sometimes uncomfortable circumstances. This dilemma has been resolved by technological advancement. Now Fans can watch their favorite artists in the comfort of their homes or any other location of their choosing. Furthermore, those deep in the rural areas that do not have the necessary infrastructure to host a music show or festival will not be left out. Virtual Reality (VR for short) is most likely going to be another revenue source for the music producers and music industry at large.

Automation will be the major tool for the music-making process.

An experiment was carried out in 2016 by the Sony group to test the effectiveness of automated music production with the use of AI (Artificial Intelligence). The result was not all that great, but the fact that a whole song was successfully produced by a computer has made this particular technological advancement the terrifying one yet. It is especially terrifying to musicians, songwriters, and music producers because record labels will discard their services in favor of AI in the event of success. Social media and streaming of songs caused A&R to be obsolete; AI promises to negatively affect the majority of the other players in the music industry.

Old genres will take a back seat while new genres will take the front seat.

There are a plethora of new and emerging music genres out there now. Genres keep evolving so much that when people are asked about their favorite genres, they cannot give a clear-cut answer. A good example is a successful marriage between hip-hop and country music evident in Lil Nas X's Old town road (2019), Adam Calhoun's clean money (2019), etc. This merging of genres to form new, fresh, and unique genres is a practice that has come to stay.

There will be no such thing as Superstar Artists anymore.

Superstar musicians like Drake, Beyonce, and Jay-Z are not only musicians, they also have their hands in all sorts of businesses, although the music was the stepping stone that put them out there and made them household names.

Upcoming artists that intend to use music to make a name for themselves have it hard as a result of the sheer number of talented musicians in the industry. Therefore, artists have to divide all their eggs into different baskets to get ahead and work extra hard even more than the "superstars" for their music to stand out, to attain superstardom, and maintain it.

Chapter Five: Making Your First Song

Making music now is the easiest it has ever been, and with the way things are going, it is going to get easier and easier. All that you may need to accomplish your music production goals are all readily available; the equipment, the passion, the talent, dedication, determination, money (might be scarce but we have found a way around that yes?), and so on. In the earlier chapters of the book, the pieces of equipment you will require for an effective home recording experience have been explicitly stated the ideal specifications and budget-friendliness. Furthermore, as a beginner, some of the relevant and fundamental information, especially on the rudiments of music theory, were also outlined, albeit sparingly detailed. The fundamentals are quite necessary for a songwriting beginner.

There is definitely a generic methodology to the music production processes; however, it is still rather quite a personalized thing. At the end of the day, you will have to customize the processes to fit you as an artist. The customization process is not something you just pull out of thin air; you gain the necessary knowledge to be able to customize by studying well established, seasoned, and professional music producers at work. Studying alone will not cut it, practicing what you learn and see matters a lot too. It is from practicing you will gain confidence, and build the ability to create your own unique music production style.

As it was earlier stated, blindingly abiding by a specific group of steps is not how you will make songs that will wow people. However, here is a guideline to serve as a canvas for you to paint your own style as the case may be. Note that all other processes/ stages are embedded in the following umbrella chapters.

- The recording chapter

- The audio editing chapter

- The mixing chapter

- The mastering chapter

The Recording Chapter

This chapter revolves majorly around writing a song either alone or with the help of other talented person/persons and simultaneously uploading the song on your well-selected DAW.

Write a Song or Get a Songwriter?

Before we get into the nitty-gritty of writing a song, it is important you understand precisely what it means. Songwriting is the process optimally combining a variety of music elements; chords, lyrics, demo track (from audio samples or an original that is, made by you from scratch), rhythm, melody, and harmony. A song inspired by an ideology, a story, and a desire to answer an unspoken question. In the past, you only needed to combine an instrument, melody, and lyrics with writing a song, but now, it is not enough to write a "good song." Any song you seek to write or have written for you must be catchy and dynamic from the beginning to the end, so you don't bore your listeners. Now to the steps;

Establish the message you want to deliver through your song. Is it about love, hate, death, sex, etc.? This will inform the initial tempo of your base track (either from a drum or a metronome)

Decide on the type of instruments to employ. Emphasis on the plural; instrument(s). We are in the multitrack recording era, after all. It might be physical instruments or virtual instruments.

With your MIDI or audio interface plugged into your computer, you can begin your recording in earnest.

For the rhythm, you record the drums, acoustic guitar, and bass. The rhythm comes first because it is made up of the traditional lead instrument in a typical musical.

The next sounds are your chords which form the harmony of the song. The instruments used here depend on the mood you want your song to present. It is the piano or the violin or ukuleles, etc.

After the chord progressions have been established, the next on the agenda is to record your melody. Melody is majorly made up of the vocal aspect of your song. This is where your lyrics come out to play, in addition to the lead guitar and background vocals. Other sounds may then be added through overdubbing. It might be sounds from samples or a particularly unique sound you already have recorded in an external drive.

The Audio Editing Chapter

Have at the back of your mind that the recording phase will not go as smoothly and as fast. You might have to record and then rerecord the tracks until they sound satisfactory. Your ears and the listening skills you acquired from listening to the pros in the game will be the judge of that. Audio editing is simply adding to and/or subtracting from your recorded tracks. The editing chapter is where you polish your tracks, so they sound great. Do not overdo it, and neither should you under do it. You must find a balance by deducing exactly where to edit. If the tracks already sound great to you, there might be no need for any major editing, just some minor fine-tuning here and there. However, if there are issues or if you would rather be thorough then:

Arrangement; this involves putting together your track one instrument after another in their respective sections (harmony, rhythm, melody, vocals). This is very necessary to prevent a drab or ludicrous sound. Arranging makes sure each chord, key, and the note is at the right section (chorus, bridge, verse) and appears at the right time in your track. It might also involve removing whole sections from the recorded track or whole reshuffling sections for conformity. In your DAW, there is an arrangement window on your timeline meant for this.

Time Adjustments; during the arrangement, the removed or reshuffled sections leave a kind of flaw that affects the real-life sound of the song if left unattended. The introduction of a crossfade takes care of it by fading down the out-shifted sound and fading up the one replacing it simultaneously.

Comping; this editing strategy is only applicable when you have duplicates or triplicates of a particular track, and you want to select the single best of them. Another comping method which involves extracting the best parts of each track and then merging them together to get the best. The method is very time consuming and is mostly adopted by professionals.

Noise Reduction/cancelation; we have established that the whole recording of the instruments is done in sections. It is typical in a home studio for there to be background noises from both within the home and outside. These noises are picked up by the Mic or other recording devices, and they end up distorting the recordings. In a standard studio or a pro studio, there is equipment such as soundproof panels, acoustic panels, pop stands, etc. Sure all these pieces of equipment prevent noise and other external noise from intruding on the recordings; they are not so crucial for a home recording studio. And besides, they cost money which a beginner that is on a budget may not have at the moment.

For a home studio, noise reduction technique in audio editing goes a long way in removing unwanted sounds from your recorded tracks.

It is important not to mix things up. The audio editing process does not technically combine all the separately recorded tracks (parts of the whole). It just polishes and cleans up the tracks separately to prepare them for the mixing chapter of the song making process.

The Mixing Chapter

The mixing chapter is actually the hub of the audio engineers. Trust me; it is not something you can completely learn and master in a few months or even a year. Even the experienced audio engineers like the late Jon Hiseman, Syd Tha Kyd, who have spent years honing their skills, do not know it all. From the word "mix" (merging different parts to make a whole), you can deduce the layman's meaning of what audio mixing is all about.

Mixing is synonymous with moving into a new apartment. The way you arrange the furniture, flowers, the color of the walls, and other knick-knacks meant for interior décor will determine if you and your visitors will appreciate it or condemn it. Mixing works this way. Furthermore, your mixing technique has to be unique so that it will conform to the message of the song.

Mixing is all about creativity; it is the major artistic ingredient in the whole song production soup. As a beginner, the foremost and advisable step to take in your mixing journey is to map a plethora of mixes. The trick is to gather as many already made mixes as possible of all your favorite genres, not to copy directly mind you, but to create a form of a blueprint which you can follow to create your own unique mixes. For an excellent result oriented mixing experience, it is recommended you try to make the following mixing process order your guideline.

Harmonizing Faders: at this stage, balance is established among the sounds from the instruments, so some instruments do not sound way higher or way lower than the others

Instrument distance and placement (Panning): at this stage, all sounds involved will be assigned their rightful places on your DAW window for mixing. The lead section has to be placed in such a way that it will be well complemented by the other track sections. Just as you place/set up the heaviest items when moving into a new house. The tracks from the heaviest instruments; drums, bass, acoustic guitar, and even vocals should be placed.

Equalization: this stage allows you to get into the hands-on aspect of your mixing journey. It majorly involves the addition and subtraction of wanted and unwanted sounds, respectively. It comprises adding, then adjusting, subtracting then adjusting. This process is repeated until all is taken care of. For more information on the technicalities of the equalization process, see chapter two of the book.

Compression: this stage is also very important. Compression exhibits the exact sound of each instrument, so each chord, key, and note sounds very clear. This then goes further to improve the overall sound.

Reverb (or any other processing effect): the unification process kicks off from this stage whereby all the instruments come together to give a somewhat complete sound with sapience.

Automation: the goal here is to cover up the fact that the song was recorded in batches. At this stage, you will be able to manipulate the software so that each section of the song can flow into the other. Success at this stage produces a complete song with no hitch or glitch.

Mixing is not for those that are faint-hearted. It takes dedication, willingness to learn, willingness to practice, and a lot of patience. There is no room for the frustration here because it is a painstaking process.

The Mastering Chapter

Technological advancement has changed the mastering processes since its inception in the 1900s and is still changing it. It is at this stage the final product is exported. Mastering involves putting some last-minute effects to the mix in order to better the state of the song. Mastering is a complicated process mainly accomplished by the engineers whose listening skills and dope equipment can pick up any flaws or errors during the mixing process. It will further increase the layer of all sounds so that they are "wet" (loud) and equal.

As a beginner, mastering should play a very small role in the whole scheme of things. The majority of home music producers focus on one song at a time; they rarely have the finances to cater to making a whole album. Based on the financial deficiency, most start-up producers suffer. It is really hard to afford the services of a mastering engineer or even make do with a mixing engineer. This option is not budget-friendly either. What home studios end up doing is focusing more on perfecting their mixing and totally discarding the mastering stage. If this works for you, that is fine, but if not, you can begin to learn mastering at your own pace. It is going to take a lot of time and energy. Even if at the end of the day, you still require additional help to get it done, the knowledge you have gained so far will work for and not against you. As the saying goes, "no knowledge is lost."

Chapter Six: Mixing

Over the years, mixing in music has evolved, and this can be attributed to the constantly changing technology and new styles of music being developed today. Mixing is the combination of individual tracks in a recording to produce a different but unique version of the song, which sounds as good as possible. In other words, mixing is the blending of different recorded tracks together through various processes such as panning, adjusting levels, time-based audio effect (chorus, delay), Equalizer, and compression.

The goal of mixing is to create your arrangement in a way that will make the different tracks relatable to each other. The final result of mixing is known as mixdown, and it is the final step before you move on to mastering. In the years past, the technique of mixing carried out is the 4-to-4 (you create additional tracks for mixing as you mix down from the one four-track machine), whereby you mix as you go along with the music. But this has changed due to access to the internet, computer, and many tracks. Once there are more tracks available and the stereo starts recording, the main focus changes to the beat of the drum instead of the bass anchoring the record.

The main change in mixing occurred in 1975 when the then-standard 24-tracks tape machine was widely used. This made mixing evolve into what it is today, and with more tracks available, the art of mixing became more complex, and suddenly it is no longer a one-man operation. Mixing became a multi-man operation that requires the assistance of different sets of hands. It now requires the producer, engineer, band members, and assistant working together in collections of different sections. Another turning point in mixing came in 2001 with the introduction of computer-based Digital Audio workstation, the presence of DAW eliminated the need for the outboard gear used in mixing, soon mixing began to take place completely inside DAW.

How to Mix your Music

Mixing, in real sense, cannot be taught. It has to be learned. Before you can become a good mixer, you would have to practice over and over again, because being a good mixer is sometimes about the total of all mixing experiences. Mixing a song depends on the musicians, Quality of the recording, the song, the musical genre as well as the arrangement. Experience is the best way to learn how to mix, try to focus on more than one musical genre, sounds, and song arrangement when mixing; this way, you can be versatile. Mixing music is subjective; for instance, many instruments can variously relate to one another, an addition, removal, or adjustment of an instrument can have a dramatic impact that will affect your listeners. Mixing is also experimental, so don't be afraid to record different mixes and create something unique with it.

Getting Started

Before you start a mix, there are several things you need to put in place to make sure your activities run smoothly.

● Choose a mixing software

This is very important, choose a mixing software that works for you, there are several Digital Audio Workstations (DAW) that you can what with, you just pick one that soothes your taste. You already learned about some in the previous chapter.

• Choose a good monitor

Monitors are very important in listening, so make sure to choose a good one. A mixer is only as good as the monitors he uses. If a mixer does not interact well with his monitor or they don't work well with the environment, all other techniques might not be of great help. When it comes to picking a monitor, there are certainly a lot of choices, but you don't necessarily need monitors that are popular or considered standard among mixers, you can get the best out of any speaker as long as it is a good one. The trick has enough listening time to get a reference point that will determine what sounds good or bad when the mix is played elsewhere. One of the advantages of the monitors being produced today is that they come with their own board amplifier, so gone are the days of worrying about powering them up with an external amp. There are several things to consider when choosing a monitor:

Before getting a monitor, listen to it: Before getting that monitor, take your time to listen to them, purchasing a monitor is serious and should not be taken lightly. There are some things you should listen for when trying to get a monitor, they are:

❖ The frequency balance, while listening to a song you are

familiar with, check whether any frequencies are magnified or attenuated. This is essential for the mid-range crossover area.

❖ Check whether the frequency balance stays the same, whether the level is quiet or loud. The lesser the changes that occur in frequencies when the level changes, the better.

❖ Ensure that the speaker has enough output level without distortion; many monitors have built-in limiters that prevent the speaker from distorting, but this also can affect how loud the speaker can get.

Your monitor should not be selected because someone else is using it: Monitors are like guitar, just because your favorite mixer is using a Yamaha HS8 does not mean it was going to work for your music. They sound produced by the monitor may not even appeal to you

When listening to monitor, use a material that you are familiar with; this way you can adequately judge what you are listening to, and if you don't have anything recorded by you, use a favorite CD that is well recorded. Note, do not use MP3, use only CDs or a playback system with good quality higher than a 24-bit source, this way, you have an idea of the frequency response of the system

You can use just about any speaker if you have used it long enough to learn its strengths and weakness. Also, having a sonic reference to compare the sound is awesome. Your sonic reference point can be your room, your car, etc. some professionals in the fields still have a go-to place to reference their work.

How to Carry Out Basic Monitor Set-Op

The way a monitor is placed can make a huge difference in the frequency balance and stereo field. Your monitor set-up should be done before you start any listening. Here are a few tips about setting your monitors

● Check the distance between monitors: Ensure that the monitors are not placed too close or too far apart, this will cause the stereo filed to smear with no clear spatial definition and if too far, the focal point will be too far behind with you not being able to hear both sides of the speaker. The rule of monitor set-up is that the speaker should be as far apart as the distance from the listening position, in other words, if you are 4feets away from the monitors, move them 4 feet apart until an equilateral triangle is formed between you and the two monitors.

● Set your monitor parameters: Monitors can have a single or wide array of parameters depending on the type, ensure that the controls for these parameters are set correctly.

● Set your monitors in the right angle: a great trick for achieving this is to place a mirror over the tweeters and adjust the speakers such that you can see yourself in both mirrors at the same time when you are in the mixing position.

Starting a Mix

Here are a few things you can do before you open your software and start mixing.

● Determine the quality you want from the song

This is the feeling you want the song to generate, sometimes, determining the quality, feeling or musical style you want is not hard, you might already have a definite sound in mind when you start recording, in fact, most composers already have a song in their head before they start recording.

• Listen to a song with similar feelings or sound similar to what you are trying to create

Listen to songs similar to what you are trying to create, preferably, you can use your studio monitor, but this should be done at a low volume so that you do not tire your ears. At this point, you are trying to familiarize yourself with tonal and textural quality of what you want to produce in your music.

• Create a rough version of your mix without the EQ and effects, and listen to it

Doing this, try to observe the mix from the perspective of an average listener and not a producer, listen to your mix in parts and as a whole, and check whether anything some parts are catchy or just off-putting. At this stage, you are not checking for production, just whether the melodies, harmonies, and instruments will grab the attention of your listener.

• Write down your ideas

After creating your rough mix, when listening through it, take note of where changes should occur, say where an instrument would fit in the mix, or where an instrument is not supposed to be. It is always better to write this down so that corrections would be done later. You are likely to get a lot of ideas when you listen through a song the first few times.

After you have carried out the steps above, it's time to move on to the real mixing. You can start by preparing your audio files for each track. Also, prepare a file that will contain all your audio files for easy navigation. This reduces the risk of errors.

How to Create a Mixing Session for your Audio

Are you unsure of how to start? Most DAWs have a nifty template that you can use, although some of them may be basic band mix templates, there are numerous templates to choose from, and if you are not satisfied with the templates, you can create your own. A good advantage of this is that it helps you develop your own style and makes it easier to start a mix from scratch. Once you're done selecting a template, start naming.

☐ Name and organize your tracks properly

Naming your tracks might seem easy and with minimal importance, but your opinion will change drastically when you need a sound from your file, and you've forgotten what you named it. If you have the recording of a drum, do yourself a favor and label it "Drum" with a word that describes the type of drum sound made in the audio. If you name it something like track 38 or simply 38, you will have a lot of difficulties finding it when you need it.

Also, organize your tracks, develop a track layout for the instruments such that you immediately know where to find a particular instrument. For someone new to mixing, you should keep it simple. Mixing software has a sophisticated organization system for tracks, so utilize it. If you can follow a kind of layout strictly, it will be easier for you to make big mix decisions.

☐ Create a color-code and symbols for your track

It is not enough that you name your track, you can also develop a color code for it, this will save you the time and trouble of having to search for a particular track. Our brain responds faster to color than to words, so color-coding your tracks and audio, you instinctively know where the tracks are. You are more likely to keep track of your work if the drums are labeled blue, your vocals are labeled yellow and your guitar green, it also makes naming easier.

☐ Adjust the track timing

No matter how great a recording session is, not all the sections of the song will be okay. On a norm, the timing of basic track is usually adjusted after a session, but if this has not been done, and you discover that you are not satisfied with some sessions, you can adjust the time. Below are some tips for time adjustment

• Don't edit by eye, rather do it by listening to your tracks, most time, perfectly line tracks may not sound right which is why listening is very important

• Don't strive too much for perfection; every beat does not have to be perfect.

• When editing, listen to the drum. This way you might not be fool into thinking the time is perfect whereas, it's not

• Tighten up a track by trimming the release, be it the vocal, the guitar or a song ending, ensure that the release is of the same length and if one is shorter than the rest, lengthened it by a time correction plug.

Comping and Arrangement

Comping is usually carried out after an audio session; it involves recording more than one musical part so that the best bit of each is taken and edited together to get the best performance. Although it is time-consuming, if you are just starting, it is not necessary to perform this comping but note, lead vocals should be built up by judicious comping. A comp is only as good as each bit that was taken. There are things to look for when you are trying to perform vocal comping; the first is to visualize what you are originally aiming for i.e., what you are trying to say and if the singer is giving you that. If you can compare your lyrics and the vocals, and you can say that it's telling you a story, then you have achieved a great performance.

Arrangement

The arrangement is one of the keys to getting a good mix. Nowadays, a typical mixing session contains a lot of tracks that will not be used in the final mix, deleting an unwanted track and arranging the rest can be very helpful when prepping your mix. Working in the audio session can become intense, but if you don't take your time with the arrangement, the final product won't sound great no matter how good you are at balancing. Arrangement of tracks can become problematic especially now that there is access to an unlimited number of tracks. it is easy to pile up musical element, and before you know it, you are left with hundreds of track to work with, before you can achieve a good balance, the arrangement has to be in excellent shape.

Mixing is subtractive i.e., a simple act of deleting or muting an instrument that does not fit well another or a particular section of the song can create a big change.

The arrangement is centered around tension and release. A good arrangement is filled with dynamic changes, loud versus quiet, full versus sparse. A good mixer knows when to create tension and release and when to emphasize it. Creating tension and release involves muting and unmuting a track, changing the level of some instrument or vocals at points within a song. Your arrangement should be written in a manner that will prevent the occurrence of conflicting instruments. This occurs when two instruments occupy the same frequency band, are of the same volume at the same time. Luckily most artists can arrange their work, which makes it easier for the mixer, but if you are working with a band that is not sure of the arrangement or is into experimenting, a lot of conflicts can occur. The mixer can rearrange the track by muting conflicting vocals or instruments and keeping what works in the mix. This way, not only is the arrangement being influenced by the mixer but also the dynamics and general development of the song too.

To understand the mechanics of arrangement, one needs to understand its element. This element varies with the genre, but the general idea is the same. Below are some of the arrangement element

● The Foundation: They are the base of a mix, they are usually made of the bass and drums but sometimes include a rhythm guitar or keyboard.

- The pad: This is a long sustaining note or chord that add glue to the arrangement. In the past, Hammond organ and Fender Rhodes were used as a pad, but this day's synthesizers are majorly being used as a pad, real strings, and a guitar power can also be used as well.

- The Rhythm: This comes from any instrument that can play against the foundation element. They are usually the tambourine, double-time shakers and congas playing the Latin feel. This element adds motion, excitement, and energy to the track

- The lead: This is the lead instrument, vocal or solo

- The fills: This element is an answer to the lead; they are instruments that occur in spaces between the lead line. It can be a solo instrument or background vocals.

Rules of Arrangement

These are some basic rules that help make the arrangement of tracks easy

- Limits the number of element: On no account should more than four elements of arrangement be playing simultaneously, as this cause confusion for the listener, and rarely should five elements be playing simultaneously.

- All instruments should be fitted in their own frequency range; otherwise, they may clash frequency –wise.

Adding Effects

Once a good balance has been achieved in your mixing, you can butter up your work by adding an effect to taste. In general, there are six principles of adding effects

- Recreate the space around a performer by imagining the performer in the acoustic phase; this method will save you time that would be wasted experimenting with different effects

- Using smaller reverbs and short delays make the track sound bigger, especially if the reverb or delay is on the stereo.

- Longer delays and pre-delays pushes the sound farther away from the listener

- Delayed timed to the tempo of the track add depth to the track without being noticeable

- When reverb is timed to the tempo of a track, it comes out smoother

- When the delay is not timed to the tempo of a track, they tend to stick out

Delays

Delay, if properly timed, can pulse and blend into a track, making the track sound bigger and deeper at the same time without drawing attention to itself.

Types of Delays

Haas effect: this delay is usually about 40millisecond or less, it is used to add a sense of spaciousness if panned opposite the source

Short delay: they are around 40milliseconds to 150milliseconds, they add double track effect

Medium delay: usually between 150milliseconds to 400milliseconds, even though it is distinct, its function is to add a sense of space around the source

Long delay: it is between 400milliseconds and 1000milliseconds. It is heard as a distinct and specific repeat,

Stereo delay: it gives room for different delay time on each side of the stereo sound field.

Reverb

This is one of the ways artificial ambiance can be added to a track in a mix; reverbs sounds smoother when timed to the pulse of the track giving it depth without sticking out, making the mix sounds polished.

Types of Reverb

● Hall

● Room

● Chamber

● Plate

● Non-linear

Panning

Panning is centered around the width of the music; it helps sound to be placed in your mix properly; this can be done either on the left or right of the stereo field. It is advisable to keep heavier or lower sound, such as the bass or kicks towards the center.

Equalizing

This is the act of amplifying, deleting, and balancing all frequencies in a mix to get your desired sound. The frequency spectrum is described as a high example snare, low example bass, and mid example high-hat. The key role of the Equalizer is to adjust the different frequency regions, the problem encounter by inexperienced engineers is the misconception that the primary function of an EQ is to improve richness, tone and the subject appeal of the instrument in a mix, but this is just a secondary function. The reason why EQ is so important in a mix is that it can be used to adjust "Frequency masking." This is a phenomenon that affects perception whenever several instruments are playing simultaneously. In other words, if an instrument possesses more energy in a certain frequency region, it desensitizes your perception of the frequency region of other instruments. The implication of masking is big because even if the individual instrument in your arrangement sounds good, there is still a need to compensate for masking between instruments to maintain their distinct tone in the final mix. You should note that the EQ settings that work for one mix will not necessarily work for another mix, there is a need to modify the settings for each song as they contain different keys, instrumentation, and vocals.

Goals of Equalization

- To make the sound of an instrument clearer and define

- To all element in a mix fit together

- To make the mix or instrument sound larger than life.

Types of Equalizers

An equalizer is one of the most useful tools in a mix, especially when it comes to adjusting the frequency for different element, there are four types of Equalizer; graphics, shelf, filter, parametric; each with its own strength and weaknesses.

☐ Graphic

The graphic EQ comes with an adjustable number of frequencies. Usually, they have between 5 and 31 frequency bands, which affect a small range of frequency. One of their main features is to remove offending frequency from the signal and to make an adjustment to the tonal quality, but its usefulness in mixing is not that pronounced.

☐ Filter

This EQ got its name from its function because it is used to filter out unwanted frequencies that are either higher or lower than the target frequency. Sometimes carefully eliminating certain frequency will improve the sound of your track, you just need to know which one to eliminate. The low pass filter is used to eliminate unwanted high frequencies while the high pass filter is used to eliminate unwanted low frequencies.

☐ Shelf

This is similar to your filter; only it affects a range of frequencies either above or below your target frequency. One of its major usefulness is to roll off the top or bottom of your target frequency.

☐ Parametric

This is the EQ majorly involved in the mixing process. With this EQ, you can select the frequency you want to change and also the range of frequencies around it. In order words, you can select the frequency and set the range (known as Q) you want to affect. Q indicates the number of octaves that will be affected by EQ, note not all parametric EQ has the same reference number for their settings. Your Q settings should be done based on what you hear in the mix, one major benefit if parametric is the ability to increase or decrease a range of frequency, this enables you to fit different instruments together in the mix. This technique is known as carving out frequencies. It is the most useful in mixing because it allows for adjustment of the frequency response of each instrument so that other sound can be clear. A major disadvantage is that some systems don't offer many bands, so your decision has to be made based on the number of available bands.

Equalizing Methods

Different engineers have different equalizing methods that get the job done, so if the method below does not work for you, just keep on trying other methods. The method does not matter, only the end result. The methods include

❖ Equalizing for definition

❖ Equalizing for size

❖ Juggling frequencies

Equalizing for definition: a well-recorded source material can sound lifeless due to some frequency that is either overemphasize or attenuated, often time, the lack of distinction of an instrument is because there are too much lower midrange frequencies usually between 400Hz to 800Hz. This adds a boxy quality to the sound; it can also be undefined because it lacks in the 3-kHz to 6-kHz area. This method can allow you to eliminate the frequency that is masking the definition of the sound. To perform this task, there are steps for it

• The boost/cut control should be set to a moderate level of cut

• Browse through the frequencies until you find the offending frequency

• Cut to taste

Note: Excessive cutting makes the sound thinner, so be conscious.

Equalizing for size: This is used to make a sound bigger or larger than life. It can be achieved by adding Bass and sub-bass in the frequency range of 40Hz-250Hz. Although the major area this occurs is below or above 100Hz or both. The step to carry out this method are written below

• The boost/cut control is set to a moderate level of boost

- Browse through the frequencies until you find the one with the desired amount of fullness

- Boost to taste

Note: Too much boost will make the sound muddy

Juggling frequencies: Soloing and equalizing a particular instrument without listening to others will become problematic; the equalize instrument will begin to conflict with other instruments when you try to improve their sound. This is why it is important to listen to other instruments while you are equalizing. Juggling frequencies make the sound fit together in the mix

Here is How it's Done...

• Start with the rhyme section i.e., the bass and the drum; each instrument should have a clear and distinct sound; if not, make sure two EQs are not boosting at the same frequency, and if they are set one to a slightly higher or lower frequency.

• Add the next most influential element, which is usually vocal, and if it is not clear, carry out the step above.

• Add the other element to the mix one after the other and check each against the previous element.

The idea is for each instrument to have a clear and distinct sound that fits together in the mix.

Equalizing Techniques

Here are some general tips

- When boosting your mix, make use of wide bandwidth and a narrow one when cutting

- If you want a sound to blend in with the mix, roll off the top; but if you want it to be distinct, roll off the bottom

- The fewer the instrument, the more distinct each sound should be and vice versa

- If your mix sounds muddy, remove 250hz, if honky remove 500hz

- Cut some elements if you are trying to make the mix sound better and boost if trying to make it sound different.

Paying for Mixing

Can't or scared of mixing your music yourself? There are several engineers that you can pay or hire to mix the tracks for you. However, there are a few things you have to consider first when hiring an engineer to mix your song. The factors you have to put under consideration are

- Style: choose an engineer that is in your genre, if you have the choice; this way, he can give you the best mix.

- Sound: before hiring that mixer, listen to his work, does it sound professional, are you satisfied with the sound. If you okay with his work, you can hire him

- Reputation: feedbacks given by other musicians that have work with this engineer will give you an idea of what to expect; also, the credit awarded to him can be of great help. Check this when you are about to hire an engineer

● Budget: mixing is usually done by songs, consider your budget before you hire a mixer

Platforms for Hiring a Mixer

❖ Fiverr

❖ Upwork

Chapter Seven: Remix

Remixing can be defined as the process of altering the original version of a song through the addition and subtraction of element, altering the tempo, dynamics, equalizer, playing time or generally any musical component of the song, in other words, remix is the creation of an alternate version of a song where instrumentation balance is different. Now, we will dive into remixing proper, but let us first take a look at how it came to be.

Before the advent of magnetic tape in 1930, record editing was not readily available. But when the electric tape surfaced, it opened people's eyes to the whole new world of creating an alternate version of songs. The world began to see the potential in it, creating this alternate version just involve cutting, adjusting, and adding to an entire performance. Another game-changer in remix occurred in the 1940s when the multi-track recorder was introduced. The first 8-track recorder was invented by Les Paul, a renowned guitarist, and inventor, but not without the help of Ampex corporation who designed it. This recorder was designed to enhance band recording with additional overdub. The capacity to separate different instruments made it possible to alternate different parts in a final recording. This caused a major turnabout for the music world, as this invention made it possible to create a sophisticated and complex recording and even make changes to it after the original recording session. This led to the birth of remix, which will later go on to be considered as an area of specialization and its own niche.

Later on in the decade, a major change would occur that would open people to the true potential of the remix world.

By 1960, the multitrack recording was well established and its true potential being explored and utilized. Modern remixing can be traced to dancehall, which originated from Jamaica; it constitutes elements of reggae, dub, ska, and rocksteady. Some pioneer producers from that time include King Tubby and Lee "Scratch" Perry. They help popularize this new brand of music, by altering the instrumentals and creating another version to sooth their audience's taste. They started by creating only vocal tracks, but it soon evolved into a sophisticated format of isolating hooks, repeating hooks, creating various effects such as delay and reverb, alternating, or creating new instrumentals. Around this same period, in the U.S, the DJs developed a way to keep people on the dance floor. They simply repeat a certain part of the song through a simple process of Tape looping and editing. A notable figure who invented the dance remix as Tom Moulton, although he was not a DJ, he started by making Mixtape for a disco dance club, this eventually became popular and garnered attention from the music industry. Studios began to employ him to improve the aesthetics of disco recording; soon, record labels began creating an alternate version of songs. Moulton would later move on to specialize in dance floor remix. As of today, many basic techniques being used today are from Moulton's works. He would later go on to invent the 12-inch single vinyl format and the breakdown section. Some other influential pioneer of the disco era includes Walter Gibbons, Tee Scott, and Jim Burgess from Salsoul records, in fact, one of the notable work of Walter Gibbons is 12-inch single (ten percent by Double exposure) which, against popular belief did not mix the record, he only did a re-editing of the original version. Prior to this period, the 12-inch single was only available to club DJs. In the 1970s, 1980s, and 1990s, the 12-inch single was a big commercial success, and Salsoul records became home to legendary remixers.

Why Remixing?

There are numerous reasons why people carry out remixing

● It helps create an alternate but unique version of the original song to suit the audience's taste.

● Remixing helps to develop creativity: remixing is a skill, and remixing a song helps you think creatively, it allows you to express your ideas uniquely.

● It gives room for the conversion of a song from one genre to another

● It helps a song reach different listeners, therefore more market.

● It brings old songs into relevance

● It helps to adapt the beat to fit dance club or radio.

● It also helps to improve/ enhance the original version of a song.

Types of Remixes

Remix can be categorized into six different type

● Official remix: This is the one commissioned by the artist or record with stem or MIDI files made available to the remixer, and this is commissioned for profit, the remixer gets a share of the profit. Often, these remix becomes more popular than the original song.

● Bootleg: Otherwise known as the Unofficial version, this remix is done without the knowledge of the artist or record label. Most times, the stem is not available to bootleggers, so they work with a DIY acapella; they usually add their own instrumentation to the song. Sometimes bootleggers can make a particular song popular e.g., Run DMC by Jason Nevins.

● Radio or club edit: creating a custom remix for radio and club helps the song to reach a broad set of audiences. It helps cut down some certain section like a lengthy intro for radios and has more drum parts for club

● Re-edit: re-editing is more popular among DJs; it could involve a full re-arrangement, removal of some verse, and lengthening of some drops to fit dance club.

● Mash-up: this involves the merging of two songs together to create a new one, it can merge the acapella of one song and the instrumental of another to give a different mix.

● VIP: This is usually created from an artist's biggest hit, they re-create the original mix but with some extra like vocals, chords, and drums.

How to Remix

Based on the fact that you are reading this book and you have gotten this far, you are interested in being a remixer. When you want to start a remix, there are certain processes and terms you need to get familiar with to be able to do your job properly. Here are the step by step guide for remixing yourself

1. Selecting the best track for the remix and the vocal extraction

2. Creating and defining keys for a remix

3. Arrangement and final adjustment

1. Selecting the best track for the remix and Vocal extraction

The first step in remixing is selecting a good track. This is one of the major factors in creating a good remix. Not only is the right track important, but the version you would be comfortable working with, besides music, is subjective in nature. It doesn't matter which genre you pick as long as it suits your purpose. When picking a classic song, select a familiar one, there are several opportunities to explore. Also, do not select a song with a popular remix.

Another factor to consider when selecting a song is the vocals. Can the vocals be easily extracted from the song? If not, creating a new vocal can take a lot of time. Extracting the vocals, if done well, have a great impact on the rest of the remix.

Finding Vocals for a Remix

The Acapella of the original song is one of the best sources of vocals, one of the sites for obtaining this is SoundCloud, but often time the acapella version is not always available, so you are left with the option of extracting it from the original version. Extracting vocals from the original version is not as hard as it sounds. There are a few ways to go about it.

● the first method is to eliminate the music bed and its instrumental counterpart

● using software and website

Eliminating music bed and the instrumental counterpart

Nowadays, songs are released with their instrumental version, which is mainly for a DJ. Some do include vocal notes but with no vocals. These vocal notes can be used by playing it against the original but in an inverted form. The easiest way to achieve this task is to use software with an inverted function. An example of this Audacity. The steps below highlight how to go about the extraction

● Load the file with the instrumental version on the software.

● Highlight the file and invert it.

● Add the vocal version on top of the inverted instrument version. The instrument in the vocal version and the inverted instrument cancel each other, leaving only the vocal.

● Edit your vocal to remove unwanted sounds such as background noise and unwanted beats.

Using Software and Websites

Some software's especially the Adobe Audition CS6, is created mainly for sound editing and will perform the above steps. They are also specially built to create acapella. It's not always that software will give you the perfect vocals, sometimes there is a need to equalize some parts, tweak a section but most importantly, you are not working blind because you can listen to what is being created.

After the extracted vocals have been properly cleaned, you can re-record it with a new vocal with a talented vocalist; you can easily get a vocalist from sites like YouTube, Looperman, and Sound cloud. Try and recreate something similar to the original version. Make sure the vocal is of good quality to prevent muddied sound later on in your remix.

2. Creating and defining keys for a remix

If you are well versed in music, you can easily get the keys. But for beginners, you can always google search the chords; they are available on several websites. The choice is yours, whether you want to work along with the original version or you want to get creative, either way, it is better to listen and play along with your naked vocal first. Also, you can play an entirely different instrument and loop it couple with your new vocal; you get a new and entirely different song. A key factor to consider is the tempo; if you are using this method, there is a need to work out the tempo difference; if not, this might result in a clashing.

How to the Find Tempo of a Song

Below is the guide to calculating the tempo in a song

- Get the pattern of reoccurrence of the steady beat

- to calculate the time; this can be done using a stopwatch,

- listen for the strongest beat, this will give you an idea of where to start if you are distracted

- Mark the number of full measures you hear every 30secsi.e when you hear the beginning of a new beat.

- Multiply the number of measure by the number of beats per measure

- Multiply the result by 2 to get the BPM

There are also software for calculating the tempo of a song

1. Mixmeister BPM analyzer

2. Online BPM calculator and counter

3. Android app, "Live BPM."

4. Logic Pro X

5. FL studio

Instead of working with loops, there is an option of building your own beat from scratch. This is very easy to achieve. There is a tool that can be used. The BTV solo is perfect for this; with this tool, you can easily build your own beat once you get your vocals; you can now load it into your preferred DAWs and start remixing. An example of DAWs that can be used for this includes Audacity, Ableton, and audition.

3. Arrangement and final Adjustment

This is the last stage in a remix; at this stage, every component is well blended together to give a nice sound; never the less, it might still need a few adjustments. Here you can add other effects like reverbs and delays. When arranging your remix, start with percussion instrument and kick drum.

A Few Tips for Remixing

- Don't overdo it and don't pressure yourself

- Don't be afraid of the track is similar to the originals, you can always find ways to improve it

- Be creative, experiment, create a signature sound that will be unique to you

- Always take time to arrange and master your song, and if you are not yet perfect in your mastering, you can always hire a professional.

Chapter Eight: Collaboration

Collaboration in music results in the creation of something unique. This is achieved when two individuals in music team-up together to produce something better than what would have been created individually. Collaboration involves the combination of each individual's knowledge, style, and creative skill in one song. This combination could be that of an artist working with a producer, the combined effort of multiple songwriters, or two artists working together.

Why do Artists Collaborate?

Collaboration in music opens doors for different opportunities, and you can easily tap into its advantages. A good example is the Beatles, which was formed in 1950 as a result of different individual teaming together. Collaboration brings together ideas and skills from different sources and combines them into one. In the world of music, people have different ways of doing things, from the producers with different ways of mixing to the songwriters with different styles of writing. Everybody has a style that is unique to them. Collaborating with others in music gives an avenue for the creation of something new and original. One of the individuals can be good in one aspect like the beat while he is not so confident about the lyrics, the other might be able to create an award-winning lyrics but sucks at the beat aspect of music. The combination of their talent can lead to the creation of something unique and original. Two minds working together are better than one, with two or more artists in collaboration, different ideas are generated, they inspire each other, together they can create something that would be a hit in the market. By having two different sets of ideas, you will have a lot of angles to explore when composing a song; also, the project will be fun and enjoyable because you are working with someone who shares your enthusiasm. You will help each other accomplished what could not be done individually; it also a source of motivation. You might not be able to recognize your flaws, but fresh eyes and ears can easily point it out. You give each other feedback and constructive criticism, how to fine-tune your idea to give the best possible result.

Another reason for music collaboration is the exposure; you can reach a new set of audience that belongs to the other artist and vice versa, especially if the collaboration is done with an artist with a different style and genre from your own. This gives you a chance of promoting yourself to potential audiences, fans, and open doors for gigs and concerts for those looking to do a live show. Collaboration can also open doors for different connections and contacts through the other artist. These contact and connection can be further used to gain more music collaboration or get you closer to being signed.

The more the number of artists in collaboration, the wider the range of the audience, the higher the promotion budget. Sometimes you might be collaborating with an artist that has a large marketing, promotion, and social media team. This can be beneficial to your collaborative track, as this can help it garner a lot of recognition.

How to Collaborate with Other Artists

To make a success of your collaboration, you need certain principles and regulations to guide you, especially if you are new to the game.

☐ Find time to interact with your collaborating artist before the session

This is crucial; the two collaborating artists need to be comfortable around each other. Spending time with your collaborating artist before the session is not a bad idea; neither is communication.

☐ Outline your ideas before the session

It is always good to prepare beforehand —the song name, chords, and lyrics, your goal for the song, and the audience you intend to reach. This way, the other artist is familiar with the idea of what the song should be; even if the idea is not the main focus of the session, brainstorming gives you a better understanding of your sound.

☐ Be open to new ideas

Remember you are working with someone with a different style and way of doing things, be open to their ideas. Even if you are not feeling it, be sure to try it first before you completely disagree. Also, when other people are bringing a fresh perspective to the song, try to look at it from their angle.

☐ Don't force ideas

If it is your first time, it is understandable if ideas are not coming because you are working outside you might comfort zone. It is always better to go over the track again than force an idea that is not working, let fresh ideas come naturally to you.

☐ Don't be discouraged, if the session does not work out the first time

Even though the session did not go the way you want, or the final product is not to your own taste, don't take it the wrong way, chuck it as a learning experience and maintain your relationship with the other artist.

☐ Be organized

Being organized helps reduce stress and helps you focus more on your session, good work ethics such as punctuality, good preparation, and integrity. This helps to foster trust.

☐ Understand individual role

Make sure everybody is clear on their role, and the quality of the song is a collective responsibility that should be taken seriously.

☐ Online tools and services for collaboration

Over the years, artists have worked together to create songs that have been a hit in the market, but now, it is made easier with technology. Technology has made it possible to reach other creative minds, whether they are in your vicinity or on the other side of the continent. Online tools and services connect you to other musicians, producers, vocalists, and songwriters. It allows you to rehearse, play, and record music with other people who share your enthusiasm. You can exchange ideas, discover new music, and experiment without the burden of renting an expensive recording studio. Online music collaboration is not a hard feat to achieve, you simply create your track, and you upload it for others to build on, and if you have a good internet connection, you can play in real-time and avoid the delay of transmitting audio on the internet. Collaboration can be public or private, depending on your production needs. The DJs and creative people are not left out as they also can use this service to create Remix and others.

Tools and Services for Online Music Collaboration

1. Tunedly: it is an online music recording studio and one of the lasted options if you are looking to collaborate. It combines file sharing with services like live chat and videos. It is one of the best platforms for finding musicians anywhere in the world. Before you can access all the incredible features, you need to create a free account. Once this is done, you can go through the numerous list of a musician on this platform and select who to work with. You can then upload your file containing stem, lyrics, and instrumental, then contact the musician either through live chat or message to brainstorm on ideas.

2. MixMatchMusic: This is a free online community for sharing ideas in music. It provides opportunities for collaboration. Through this platform, you can connect with different people to create, remix, and complete your song through the audio tool possessed by MixMatchMusic. To

get a musician to collaborate with, you can upload your tracks and look for the right musicians, don't forget to check their ratings. Another feature of this platform is the ability to publish your finished work on the platform and get paid.

3. Kompoz: This platform has a cloud-based workspace tool through which you can connect with other musicians and producers for your work. In this platform, you also get paid for your finished result if it is published and sold. You can upload your tracks and invite others to work on it, and if you need feedback on your song, it has a forum discussion, music can be produced under a creative commons license or traditional copyright if you want to retain sole ownership.

4. Blend: This platform is impressive. You can put your work song out there for anybody to work on, or you can select the set of people that will be working on the song. You can also use bit and pieces from the remix to build the original version. A good advantage of this is the online backup it provides for your DAWs

5. Vocalizr: This varies a bit from the rest; it connects producers as well as vocalists together, if you require a good vocal, this is the best option for you.

6. Audiu: This is a perfect forum for collaboration, with their new community-focused iOS and android app, you can reach out to more musicians anywhere.

7. Splice: This Platform is becoming popular with music producers due to the many amazing features it possesses, like its counterpart Kompoz, it is also a cloud-based tool,

but splice is built solely for remixing and collaboration. It is also great for downloading plug-ins. Some of its features include online back-up, version control, visualization of the creation process, offline, and online backup.

Tips for Online Collaboration

Online collaboration without proper planning or suitable platform can turn out to be a huge waste of time; whether you are trying it for the first time or you have done it before, there are some guiding principles you can follow to get the best out of your collaboration project

❖ The key is good and accurate communication: technology has made collaboration easy, quick, and convenient, but this does not mean that the message always conveys the exact information we want to get across. It is common for misunderstanding and misconception to occur, and this can hinder the project and the expected result you want. To avoid this, you need to define your song and outline the message you want to pass across, be clear on the genre as these collaborators are influenced by this, also, give them a reference song and rough draft. This provides a starting point and also an idea of what the song would be.

❖ Select a suitable File-sharing service: There are several options available when you want to choose a platform for collaboration, there are also some tools that provide good file-sharing services such as Dropbox, Goggle Drive, and OneDrive. This platform allows you to correspond with anyone that has an email. It also permits them access to files required to put the song together. This can be a wav.

File or lyrics sheet that will be accessible to all parties for modification and editing depends on an individual's role in the song. This service allows all parties involved to see how changes are being carried out; some offer live chat to facilitate good communication. Those involved in the collaboration must stick to one of the services and are familiar with the features. Remember, each service has its features and benefits, so it will be advisable to discuss beforehand on which one to choose.

❖ Be straightforward about who owns what: This is one of the important facts that must be discus among the collaborators or any other musical partnership. It a common occurrence for numerous vocalists, composers, and producers to receive credit for a song. The purpose is to know who should receive royalty, payout, and how much when the final project is released commercially. Well, the more the people working on a collaboration project, the less they will earn for their input when compared to one with fewer people, there is the need for them to discuss the percentage they are willing to settle for when the song is released. This will help prevent future conflict and lawsuit, especially if the song becomes a hit. Platforms like Tunedly can be handy in this type of situation; it protects music creators as all services are provided in the "work for hire" agreement. This is beneficial if you need a collaboration for your song but still want to retain a larger percentage of ownership.

❖ Be creative: With online tools, it is easy to be flexible and creative with no restriction that is usually associated with music studios. One of the main benefits is that it facilitates the exchange of ideas with different types of people, even though you might be in different parts of the world. It brings a fresh perspective into play so you can explore a new and different angle from what you usually do. However, you have to be careful because some people have a strong personality that can overshadow others. This could cancel the whole point for the collaboration. The most important thing is to ensure that the final song has a distinct voice and brand.

❖ Work with professionals: For a successful collaboration, the partners must possess the required expertise and equipment to be able to fulfill their role. You don't want to entrust your project to someone who lacks the skill or equipment to build your song, especially if you are paying for the services or giving up some of the ownership. Besides, listeners prefer good quality audio where the vocal, instrument, and lyrics will be distinct and enjoyable, and if you plan on pitching the song, the first thing record label look out for is a clean, professional sound. With a competitive market, the good quality sound will stand out before you collaborate with People, check their skills through bios, reviews, and past work.

Chapter Nine: Branding Your Music

Branding is what makes you distinguishable from others, think of it as your reputation. It is a way of reaching a specific audience to create a perception about you. A lot of musicians feel that their music is the most important asset, well it is true, but your music is only important if you can get people to listen to it. Without that, you have no music. There is a wide ocean of talent out there, but a musician that takes his time to effectively communicate what his music is about and what makes it different from the others is likely to stand out. When you effectively communicate what you stand for, even before people listen to your music, you are on your way to building a loyal fan-base, and branding is the key to achieving that. Note, your brand is not just about your music alone; it encompasses what you stand for, your belief, and your idea.

The Brand Component

A brand is made of two-component

1. The brand identity

2. Brand image

Brand identity: This is what you stand for; it is the combination of your core values and beliefs that you project to the world. It is an aspect you can control.

Brand image: This is how you are being viewed by the general public, including your audience. You have no control over your brand image, but you can influence it. Your brand image varies since different people see you from a different perspective.

Branding is made up of two parts, the active and the passive. Passive branding does not bring direct interaction with your audience; they are Stagename, logo, music, physical appearance, and style, while Active branding involves direct interaction with your audience. It helps influence the way people perceive you and also reinforce your connections with your fan. It includes: what you stand for, what you do, what you post on social media.

How to Create a Brand for your Music

Creating a brand does not happen overnight; it requires strategic planning and preparation. This process might take years to achieve, or it could take months, depending on your effort. The first step to creating your brand is defining it; you have to know what your brands stand for, the message it passes across to your audience. You can start by answering the following question, what inspires you, what genre is your music, how do you want people to feel when they listen to your music.

How to Create a Music Brand

☐ Create a brand vision: The first step you can take is creating a vision, you can use this set of questions to get your answer, for example, how do you want people to see your brand, what does your brand stands for, answering these question might give you an idea you want.

☐ Develop self-awareness: As an artist, it is important to understand yourself and know who you are, to understand yourself, you need self-awareness. Self-awareness is not something that occurs overnight; rather, it has to be developed over some time. Some aspects of who you are can be the foundation of your brand. Developing self-awareness is not an easy task as it is a product of all our life experiences, environmental and cultural influence, social interaction. The better you know yourself, the faster you can figure out what makes you different, and this will be good for the brand.

☐ Establish your Brand identity: once you have a clear understanding of who you are, you can now establish a brand identity. People have different beliefs, interests, goals, experiences, and values. Decide what approach or angles that will be the foundation of your brand identity. This will make it easier for people to associate with your identity. Some examples of branding angles include sex symbol, love, and relationship, sexual orientation, race and ethnicity, childhood experience, highly accomplished (competition winner), mysterious or elusive, Romance, and lifestyle. Mind you; you can always explore more than one angle for your brand identity. Sometimes your brand identity might not necessarily be who you are. It can be a character or persona that is made up not in any way similar to your true self. Establishing a brand identity does not mean you can't represent yourself in other ways different from who you are. Some artists that have been able to build a brand through this method include Lady Gaga, KISS, Gorillaz. Moreover, the purpose of building an identity is to have something unique for people to connect with emotionally.

☐ Identify your target audience: after your Brand identity has been established, the next step to market yourself. You should know that without a targeted audience, marketing may not be effective. Sometimes your target audience might share something in common with you. Furthermore, with a target audience, there is a better chance of knowing what they want, so catering to their needs will be easy. To begin marketing to your audience, you have to know how to identify them. To do this, you have to understand there believe, their interests, how they see the world and where they spend their free time.

☐ How to reach your target audience: once you have identified your target audience and you have a good understanding of their needs. There are several online tools and social media platforms that can be used to reach your audience. Some of these include Facebook, SoundCloud, Reddit, and blog post. With all these vast online tools, you can streamline the type of people you want to meet.

☐ Start Branding: once you have been able to achieve everything above, it is time to start branding. This includes sharing posts on social media and doing things in real life that resonates with your brand image and identity. Branding is in two parts, as discussed earlier in this chapter; it can either be passive or active. Branding is a gradual process, it is not a failure when money is not quickly generated, but as long as you are connecting with your target audience and building trust, it's fine. Since branding does not have a standard method of quantification, the number of people willing to pay to see your performance shows how effective you are with your brand. In other words, your branding effort will determine how the crowd responds to you.

How to Promote your Brand

As a musician, there are several ways to promote your brand once it is created.

1. Create a website: Certain platforms provide a template on how to create a website; a notable example is WIX. You can use your website to promote your music. Your fans should be able to contact you through your website, download your songs, and buy tickets for upcoming shows.

When creating your website, ensure that it reflects your brand identity.

2. Utilize social media: one of the fastest ways to promote your brand is through social media. Social media give you access to a large audience. Share posts that resonant with your brand, engage your followers, ask for their input, create competitions. Doing these will get the attention of your target audience.

3. Collaborate with influential artists: another way to promote your brand is to collaborate with other artists that are already successful in the industry, this gives you access to a different fan base and audience. The collaboration can be with an artist from your genre or another genre; either way, it can help boost your brand. Apart from collaboration, you can also promote your brand if you are featured in a very influential music blog, podcast, interview, or radio station.

Developing your Sound

Before you can become a successful artist, whether you are a DJ, a songwriter, or a vocalist, there is a need for you to market your music. A successful artist is not defined by their song alone but by the image they project as well. But before you can brand your music, you must develop a sound, unique to you; this is your signature sound. When you develop a recognizable sound that is your signature, you will easily stand out in the crowd. Mostly, an artist's signature sound is 90% copied and 10% original; creating your signature sound is a very important duty for any artist, not only for branding but also for an artistic reason. The problem with modern musicians is that they are always trying to find common ground for what fulfills them and what makes them stand out. Below are ways to develop your sound

- Follow your idol but carefully

It is okay to be inspired by an artist or try to emulate them, but be careful before you blend completely with their style, Nowadays, upcoming modern musicians think they should imitate the hottest artist on the scene. It is good to emulate your idol, however, don't emulate it so much that their image and yours cannot be differentiated. While it is good that they are your source of inspiration, it is better to concentrate on how they inspire you and what you can take from their style. It is not uncommon to modify an artist's style of music.

- Fail to get better

The journey has to begin somewhere. Don't forget you are new to this; it may take a while, but keep on building yourself until you get there. Artists that are successful today all have old demo and song that are good, but because it was the early stage of their career, did not make it to the market.

- Don't be repetitive, be consistent

Consistency is one of the keys to building your sound, and it takes a lot of practice, incorporate your style into new ideas, as a musician, you need to evolve but with your signature sound. It is cool when a fan can say, "this is artist A."

- Make use of technology

Experimenting with technology can give you an idea of your sound. Try messing around with music production tools; this was how rock music was born by playing guitar through a broken amplifier. Sometimes this helps to develop your sound.

• Combine two genre or re-inventing older sound

You can experiment with two different genres of music and see where it takes you or take an old song and recreate it to suit your taste.

• Build your dynamics

Master the use of dynamics and effect; they prevent a song from sounding monotonous.

• Be unique in your arrangement

The way you arrange your song, your rhythm, and your groove help define your music.

• Find your influence, let it reflect in your music; this takes you closer to developing your sound.

Chapter Ten: Getting Feedback For Your Song

Feedback is one of the best ways of improving your songs. This aspect of music is essential to the improvement of an artist; it helps to improve your music and production skills. As artists, sometimes, we are so immersed in the production that we don't see what is wrong with a song until we seek other opinions. Another set of ears and opinions will bring a fresh perspective to the song. Positive and negative feedbacks provide a new angle; they let you make good artistic decisions and gives you new ideas on how to modify a song.

Types of Feedback

There are three common types

● Technical feedback: This feedback is specific; it is also the most useful because it involves people with a particular skill giving you advice on the technical aspect of your song. Their advice is constructive showing you where there is a need for adjustment to bring the best out of your song e.g., a mixing engineer giving advice on arrangement

● General Feedback: the advice given is general unlike the technical feedback that gives specific advice; moreover the advice is for making artistic decisions e.g., adding vocals

● Opinion feedback: this feedback is the most common but also the hardest to apply, it let you know about people's opinion on your song, whether it is good, and they like it or bad.

Asking for Feedback

The interpretation you give to feedbacks matters a lot. Some online services provide a platform for obtaining music feedback, and this allows you to obtain constructive and useful feedback without annoying other people.

How Do You Ask For Feedback?

1. Know the reason why you want feedback on the song: Why are you sending this particular song? Is it because you are stuck and out of ideas, or you are having a difficult time deciding what to do with the song? Do you have so many ideas for the song that you need help deciding which of the ideas would work? These are some of the reasons for sending a song for feedback.

2. Give others thoughtful feedbacks: If you want good feedback on your song, extend the curtsey to others. According to Sound Cloud, the best way to gain followers on their site is to interact and provide feedback for other musicians. If you give a thoughtful comment on their song, the higher the chances of you getting good feedback from them. Remember, people have different tastes and preferences, the song may not be from your genre, but that does not stop you from giving good advice.

3. Ask for feedback from the right person: Sometimes, there is need to send a song to a particular person because of their skill in certain aspect, this can be for technical advice, for example, you need a feedback on your lyrics, approach a songwriter, that being said, don't overlook advice from non-musical people, they can point you to a

new angle you have not to explore yet. It is not compulsory to ask people with a musical background.

4. Know the aspect where the feedback is needed: Mostly when you ask for feedback, it is only given on one aspect or at most two. It is important to be specific about the aspect of the song where the advice is needed. Indicating this is better than getting general feedback like "this song is cool" without comment on the mix or the lyrics. This is more useful than general feedback; it gives direct information on which aspect to improve, unlike general feedback that can be overwhelming and long without useful info.

5. Ask for honesty: whenever you are sending a piece of music for feedback from friends or family, ask for honesty, you are never going to improve if they are giving you biased feedback. Sometimes honesty hurts, but it is better to improve on your music.

6. Know the emotion you are trying to convey: when you are asking for feedback, which emotions do you want the song to evoke, is it happiness, sadness, and anger. Asking the listeners what they feel when they listen to the song, this will determine whether the song is conveying the emotion you are trying to project. You should also prepare for bias comments because people's tastes are different but are sure to let them know the emotion you are trying to convey.

7. Know the commercial purpose of the song: when asking for feedback, indicate the commercial intent of the song. Is it being released for club play or radio? For someone who is not into the radio or club scene, you may not get

reasonable feedback from them. Knowing the reason can influence the feedback from the listeners.

8. Be professional when asking for Feedback: when asking for feedback, keep it simple and straight-to-the-point, if you are sending an email, it should be polite and not too wordy. Don't forget to thank people for their time.

9. Learn how to respond to criticism: As an artist, we take our work seriously and put all our effort into it. Moreover, it is not every day we get good feedback on our music; a bad comment can be a blow to us. The way we respond to this criticism matters a lot. The first thing to do when you get negative feedback is to check whether the person has a point. You won't get truthful feedback if you get defensive and act like you are being attacked when people give their honest opinion. Thank the person for their time; the good thing is you don't have to take their opinions to heart.

Where to get Feedback

Now that you know how to ask for feedback, the next step is where you can get feedback for your music. Some websites, blogs are designed for this; also, you can ask your mentor or some music influencers.

1. Online forum and websites

Online forums and websites are one of the best places to get feedback, different people will voice their opinions, and this can be of huge benefit if you know how to utilize these tools. When asking for feedback online, make sure it is written in a nice way that will get people's attention, remember you are not the only one trying to get feedback so when you join these forums, make sure you are actively contributing to it. Also, find a music forum that fits your style of music; this way, you know you are getting accurate feedback for your song. But the internet is not softhearted; sometimes it can be harsh and insensitive, be prepared for when the internet will show its harsh side.

Online Forums for Feedback

• Demo drop: this is a platform for musicians where you can submit your track for feedback and get support from another musician, artist, and producers as well. Some of the features include being able to see which of your submission garner the most support and which was the most downloaded.

• Synthshare: This is a community that allows music lovers to come together, share ideas, and get feedback. Synthshare was specially launched to give constructive criticism to musicians. The feedback on this platform is moderated to keep unhelpful and spam comments in check. The user is advised to post a thoughtful and relevant comment. You can use the review to improve your music and refine your musical concept all users are also encouraged to give feedback, the more you do this, the more you earn credit that can be used to unlock reviews for your track. Feedbacks are also rated on how helpful they are to the artist.

• Facebook groups: Facebook provides a platform for everything, it is also a popular spot for musicians to get together and share music, and it is advisable to join a private group as most public groups are filled with spam, some of this private group are hidden, and you might need an invite to join. These private groups are usually moderated.

2. Music blogs: some blogs are designed solely for music, so keep an eye out. Send out your songs to a different blog, and you may get feedback in return, some blog may post

the song if it is good, for a blog like Submit Hub, there is guaranteed feedback after payment of a token.

3. Music Professionals: There are professionals in the industry that are trained to listen to your music and give you feedback but with a certain amount of money. For upcoming artists, this might be expensive. If you have the money, you can just do it. Some of the platforms in this category include TAXI and Music Xray.

Chapter Eleven: Mastering In Music

Mastering is the last step in the finalization of audio recording, and if done correctly, it can turn your good song into a great one. The aim of mastering is to ensure proper translation i.e., all the sonic elements in the stereo mix must be balanced and the sound uniform across all platforms. Mixing involves working with individual tracks, but with mastering, you are working with the stereo mixes. Mastering is not hard to understand; in fact, it involves you working with equipment that you have already used. Whether your recording and mixing were done perfectly in an expensive studio or it was done in a less than ideal environment. Mastering is the process that involves preparing your music for final duplication. Mastering as an audio recording process did not appear until the advent of magnetic tape. Before the advent of mastering, the art of recording, mixing, and mastering was one giant process. Engineer set up a mix, play it through a disk cut with grooves using a mastering Ianthe. But because of the invention of the magnetic tape, engineers were able to separate the three processes of mastering, mixing, and recording into three different processes and not just a huge one process. Both the mixing and recording process involves sound while the mastering process is more of how the disk is cut, the running time of the disk and how much material could fit into the disk. Mastering engineers use a process like compression, EQs, sequencing to control the audio content to make cutting into the disk easier. Over the years, it has been discovered that carrying out this process on the final mix enhances the sound. The invention of CDs took mastering to a new level; this makes the task easier as there is no need to cut into a disk again.

Vital Processes Involved in Mastering

☐ Compression: Some song sounds better when smooth, while some sounds better when it has a paunchy ring to it; compression can be used to produce these effects. The addition of compression is an art in the mastering process because you have to know the amount and the type of compression to add, too little or too much compression could lead to your music sounding flat or weak. Good mastering engineers know when to make the mix sound smooth or paunchy.

☐ Limiter: The function of a limiter is to tame any instrument in a mix that is too loud compared to the rest. This is done so that the difference between the song peak level and the average level is optimal; this difference varies with the style of music, the difference is usually between 12db and 8db but must not be less than 6db.

☐ EQ: Due to the fact that each song has been recorded and mix individually over a period of time, each song probably has a different tonal quality; some may be brighter, other heavier on bass, but one thing is sure, they all have a different sound. When you are compiling your songs, their Tonal quality needs to be consistent; Your songs don't necessarily need to have the same sound, but the goal is for your songs to work well together.

☐ Sequencing: it involving arranging your songs in the order that suits your taste. Sequencing is one of the most vital aspects of mastering. You have to set blank spaces between each song so that they flow well on the CD.

☐ Leveling: This is another vital aspect of mastering, all songs have to be on the same level, and this can be done in this phase; consistency in the level of your songs helps with the flow and cohesiveness of the CD. This is achieved through compressors, limiters, and gain adjustment.

Mastering: Getting Started

As a beginner, there are guidelines that would save you a lot of time and energy if followed properly during the mixing process.

☐ Listen to your mix quietly to make sure that all the instrument and in place and not out of the mix, also ensure that the level is balanced. You can burn your song on a CD and test it against another system, e.g., boom box, to check whether the bass drum is louder than the rest or whether your song volume is high enough.

☐ Make sure you equalize all your instruments even though the entire song will still be equalized by the mastering engineer. If your instruments are not well equalized, it will affect the mastering process; for example, if your bass guitar sounds muddy and needs to be equalized during the mastering process, it could result in loss of the low end on all the instruments, this makes the mix sound thin. If proper Equalization was done in the first place, this could be avoided.

☐ Apply compression to your mix to see what it sounds like in the compressed form, mind you; in this stage, it should not be recorded yet, that is for the mastering engineer to do. By doing this, you can be able to detect whether some instruments are too loud because they become more obvious when compressed.

☐ Text the mix in mono (combining two-channel in stereo into one), you will be able to detect whether an instrument tonal characteristics is out of balance with the others. You should always monitor your mix in mono.

☐ Check for phase hole; it occurs when an instrument is recorded in stereo, and the two tracks are out of phase. To check for phase-hole, listen to the way instrument sound in the stereo field, when you have sound coming from the far right or far left of the stereo with no sound from the center, you have a phase hole. If this occurs, reverse the phase on one of the two-channel for the particular instrument. Even though mastering brings out the best in your song, don't rely on it to correct all your mistakes. Ensure that your song sounds good enough during mixing, not only does it make mastering easier, it brings out the best in your song; otherwise, the end result for the song may not be good.

Step-by-Step Guide on How to Master your Own Solo Project

Mastering your music gives you control from start to finish while saving money at the same time. There is a couple of approaches to take; you can do a CD mastering or make an MP3 file from your 24-bit mix. Some major issues with CDs are that they are 16-bits and can be truncated. But CDs is the most basic approach to mastering especially if you are mastering your song

Step 1: Select a Digital Workstation

We have learned how DAWs works earlier; Logic Pro is DAW that is specially designed for mixing; however, there are some DAWs specially designed with mastering in mind. Few of them are listed below with some of their key features

• Sequoia: it is one of the most comprehensive mastering software, a bit on the expensive side, but it has features that will give you your money worth. Some of its key features include an object-based approach to editing, which gives flexibility and ability to edit small sections of your track, MP3/AAC previewing which allows you hear how your song will sound when it is encoded in an MP3/AAC file and Spectral editing which is good for cleaning up unwanted song.

• Wave Lab Pro: it is also specialized software for mastering, it is specially built for those after precise, high-quality audio, it spectral editing function features viewing mode called wavelet display that allows your audio to be displayed through pitch scaling. Wave Lab also provides you with tools for polishing and finalizing mastering.

• Nuendo: it offers the same services as that of Wave Lab, but without Spectral editing, it offers good designs when working with surrounding mixes and 3D audio. While it might not be most favored among mastering engineers, it is good as a post-production DAW when working on an uncommon mastering project.

• Reaper: For a beginner, Reaper is one of DAW that will save you some cash, also if you are looking for a DAW that comes with Plugin, again reaper should be your choice when looking for quality tools for your project that will cost you almost nothing, this software is for you. Apart from having its own plugin, it also supports several third-party plugin; it has JSFX plugin that allows you to write your own custom plugin, which can be simple or complex depending on your project need.

Other software includes Acon Digital Acoustica Premium, Sound forge Pro, Sound blade.

Step 2: Prepare your Mix

When preparing a mix for mastering, it must have a maximum peak of 3dBFS, and this can be achieved by adjusting the master fader during mixing until 3dBFS appears on the peak meter. This is a preventive measure to guide against clipping. Also, adding a limiter will provide an idea of how the mix will sound during mastering; however, it should be removed before mastering.

Step 3: Export your Mix to Stereo

There different ways for mastering a mix, but for beginners like you, it would be easier to export your mix to uncompressed stereo format such as wav; this will ensure that the quality does not reduce before mastering. Using higher resolution for your audio preserves the information in the audio file, and there is a higher chance of the computer processing it accurately. The key is to use the highest resolution audio; this way, the quality of the track will be preserved. Note, always use24-bit for mastering (not 16-bit), the only time 16-bit should be used is when exporting your final master.

Step 4: Fix any Residual Problem

The foundation on which you are building your mastering is very crucial because it determines the end product of your mastering. Problems like over-compression, low-end rumble excess noise should be dealt with before you start mastering the tracks.

Step 5: Enhance your Dynamics

This is where that actions really take place, this stage is where you can make or mar your song, but before you panic, know that you can always re-do the process, this will only be possible if you make backup copies of your file. Note, always back up your files. The style and arrangement of your music will determine the enhancement that will be done. When it comes to enhancing your music, there are two main tools – a compressor and a limiter, and each has its function.

Tips on How to Use a Compressor and a Limiter

• With compressor less is better, use a compression ratio between 1.1: 1 and 2:1

• Always apply 1-2dB of compression or limiting at one time, if you apply more than this at a time, it will lead to artifacts (audible changes which occur as a result of over-compression or over-limiting)

• make use of a multi-band compressor to bring out each instrument in the mix

• Be sensitive to your attack and release; the short attack takes the punch out of your music while long release makes the vocal dynamics disappear.

Step 6: Perfecting your Tonal Balance

Tonal balance is how the frequencies of a song are related to one another; here you are concern with the balance of frequencies within the hearing spectrum. When adjusting the tonal balance, look for frequencies that are too loud or too soft, and this can be done using parametric EQ, the same EQ adjustment must be made on both left and right channels to keep the stereo balance intact. Any adjustment made to EQ during mastering not only impact frequency, but it also alters the whole frequency spectrum and the relation among all the instruments. Be careful when adjusting, and don't add more EQ if you don't like what you hear.

Step 7: Sequencing your Songs

Sequencing is the act of arranging your song on the CD and the amount of silence between them; in order, word sequencing is what makes your album flow. It is one of the most intuitive and relatable parts when working on an album. It includes crafting fade-in and outs, the amount of silence before a track, selecting the order in which the music will be released. The main goal of sequencing is to define the relationship between each song. The artistic part of sequencing is the time between the ending of one track and the beginning of another song. Your sequencing will determine how your album will create an impact and for how long.

Guidelines for Sequencing

• Start with the most impactful track: this is important for inviting your listener; your lead track should be impactful because it is the one that will create the first impression, and this matters a lot.

• When sequencing, think about each song's tempo. Some CDs work best when songs with similar tempo are arranged together while some are when songs with contrasting tempo are placed together.

• Consider the way each song is related lyric-wise; this is important, especially if you are trying to tell a story with your CD. Arrange your song in the order that can best tell the story

• Put your singles first, that is, if you have an already released song in the market. Listener connects more with what they are familiar with.

How to Sequence Album in DAW

Now that you have an idea of your arrangement, it's time for them to be arranged in your digital work station. This is better achieved by bringing all your songs into a new DAW session. This makes it easier to change order, add gap, and fades. Here is how to use a DAW to create a perfect sequence flow

1. Add silence: in sequencing, silence is as important as the sound; it helps you to create pacing for your album. A longer period of silence between album can be used to divert attention from two songs that are similar while a short period of silence is used to make an effect last longer

2. Add fade: this is one of the basic functions performed by the DAW, in order to enhance your sequencing, you need to understand how fades works. If properly done, it can give your album a dramatic flair. There is no exact rule guiding fade; it just requires flexibility. When using fade, the best advice is to listen. Experiment with different styles.

3. Concentrate on listening: when sequencing, listen carefully for clues on how to treat your silence. DAW provides a visual reference that can make you concentrate more on how they look rather than how they sound; it is best you close your eyes when trying to determine silence. Be careful not to pick the wrong gap; sequencing is about the feel of the song, use it

4. Counting beat to determine silence between tracks is a great way of adding rhythm to your silence, this sustains the energy between tracks with a similar rhythm, but one main disadvantage is that it becomes predictable.

There is the assumption that there is a set amount of time between all songs, well this is not true, you can set amount of silence between your tracks as long as it feels right with you.

Step 8: Balancing the Levels in your Album

This is very easy to achieve, you can balance level by playing one song after the other and listening for a significant volume difference, you don't want your listener to have to adjust their stereo volume each time a new song comes into play. If there is any noticeable difference, just adjust the volume until they are fairly the same

Step 9: Preparing for CD

After your album has been sequenced, balanced, and optimized, the last step is to save it in a format that enables duplication. The easier format for duplication is the Red book audio CD-R. When mastering your music, it must be in a 16-bit, 44.1 KHz format. If you are recording at a higher resolution, this for people using a newer hard-drive recording system, your song needs to be translated from the higher resolution rate to the CD rate. This process is referred to as dithering.

Paying for Mastering

Hiring a professional to master your music has some added advantage; you get a fresh set of ear and advice. If you don't have equipment capable of performing the level of mixing you want, you can hire a professional to do it for you.

When hiring a professional, there are tips that will help you in choosing the best one for your project

1. Check whether the mastering engineer has master songs similar to your own

2. Both you and the engineer should agree on the fee before working together. Some engineers charge per hour, while for some, you pay for the materials

3. Discuss your expectations and desire for the song; this way, the mastering engineer can master your music to your taste.

4. Take CDs whose sound is similar to what you are trying to achieve, see if the engineer can get your music to sound the same.

5. Try as much as possible to be present at the mastering session; if you are present during the session, you can easily communicate what you want.

Chapter Twelve: Sending It Out There

As an aspiring musician, even if you create good music, it won't be heard until it is out there. Sometimes you need huge support to get it out there; there are several ways to garner support for your music, and how you go about it also matters a lot. There are several platforms that allow you to build post your song and build your career from scratch. It has been discussed in earlier chapters about how they can be used to promote your music; such platforms include Sound Cloud, YouTube, Facebook, Twitter, and so on. On these platforms, you get feedback that can help in improving your music.

Guidelines on How to Get your Music out There

1. Create your image: this has been extensively discussed earlier in this book, create an image that will make you stand out. Be up-to-date with the current trend; find out what attracts people to you and magnify it.

2. Create a demo: your demo is your calling card, make sure you them ready when you are performing any gigs, ensure that your demo is of the highest quality, if not people will think you are an amateur, when recording your demo, make sure it sounds exactly the way you want it and keep it short, people don't want to listen to an excessively long demo, your demo should have a maximum of five songs. One good advice is to put your best song; first, you want to get the attention of the listener and let the cover of your demo reflect your personality.

3. Create your own website: this will help you showcase your music. Your websites should contain your bio, contact info, the latest release, and videos of live performance.

4. Social media: this is one of the best media for sending your music out there, through social media, you can get access to a lot of listeners as well as musicians alike

5. Music sites and blog: Put your music on site that will make it easily accessible to people. Sites such as iTunes, Bandcamp, and ReverbNation, this site are good at marketing your music and getting it out there

6. Secure gigs: Secure gigs by contacting booking agents in your area, submit your demo and website link to access your music, if it fits there venue, you might get hired, and this can provide exposure for your music.

How to Get Signed by a Record Label

Getting signed by a record label requires hard work and consistency. Before you attempt to send your music to a record label, make sure it sounds awesome and get feedback. There might be some ideas that will boost the track, and this can only be gotten if you seek other people's opinions.

The first step to getting signed is writing a good Bio; this can be done by utilizing online tools and platforms. Your brand should be properly represented and be consistent with the way you project your brand image. Always post new content, be active on your social media platform.

The second step is preparing your tracks. Remember you are trying to get signed, quality is the key, let your demo be of the highest quality, and must be professionally created. You would interest the label if you give them a quality demo, coupled with good music, you might just be on your way to getting signed. The content must be original, including the mixing and mastering of the tracks, the frequency should be clean, and it must not be over-compressed because you need it to be loud. Do your research, create a list of who to contact and who is interested in your music, quick advice, Only send your demo to a label that will give it actual consideration, be focused, and familiarize with the label's catalog. This will benefit you when you are trying to pitch your demo. Start small pitch your demo to record label, one at a time, don't be upset if you are rejected, it is better than no response at all. Use a spreadsheet to keep track of all your contact.

Conclusion

Finally, the journey has come to an end. Music production is not a hard task to achieve, and it just requires patience, concentration, and a little flexibility in some parts. Music production encompasses a whole lot of processes, all of which are crucial steps toward the making of your first music. However, processes like mastering and remixing are very vital in music production, including the software that is used to carry out the processes.

This book is designed to help those interested in music production but has no little or no music background. Well, here is good news. Without a music background, you can still record and produce your own music, and how do you go about that? Everything is included in the book.

As someone who is aspiring to be a music producer, this book shows you how to aggregate all the processes to give something unique and beautiful, how to get your own sound, utilize it to produce something different. Some of the topics covered by this book include:

- Mixing your music

- Mastering your music

- How to start your home recording studio

- Remixing songs to create something different

- How to Collaborate with another artist

- Branding and marketing your music

- Beginners software and plug-in

- How to get signed

This book has provided a guideline for achieving these processes listed above and simplifying it so that you don't have difficulty carrying out this music production process. Furthermore, if you have been able to get what you want from this book, there is no need to follow or the guideline strictly. These guidelines are provided to help you, once you are familiar with all the steps, you can introduce incorporate certain flexibility to your process.

This book is aimed at getting you started, even if you have little to no idea of music production. With all this process above, you will be able to start your music production from scratch. Solutions have been provided within the book to some of the possible problems you may encounter.

Finally, if you have gotten to this point, that means you are on your way to becoming a good musician or artist. Don't be discouraged if you don't get it at once; remember it's all part of the experience. You can only get better with continuous practice. Stick to what you are doing and strive to make something unique. With all this, you might just be the guy that will create the next market HIT!

References

https://www.goggle.com/amp/s/m.wikihow.com/Get-your-songs-out-there

https://heroic.academy/unconventional-guide-getting-signed-record-label/

https://www.landr.com/how-to-mix/

http://dottedmusic.com/2015/marketing/get-your-music-heard/

https://spinnup.com/blog/collaborating-with-other-musicians/

https://www.musical-u.com/learn/5-best-practices-for-online-song-collaboration/

http://blog.sonicbids.com/how-and-where-to-get-the-most-constructive-feedback-on-your-music

https://spinditty.com/industry/How-to-remix-a-song-in-3-easy-stepsBranding guide for musicians by David Nguyen

The mixing engineer's handbook by Bobby Owinski

Mixing secrets for the small studio by Mike senior

Home recording for musicians for dummies by Jeff Strong

Audio effects, Mixing and Mastering by Metin Bektas

10 Trends That Will Reshape the Music Industry

https://musicindustryblog.wordpress.com/2019/04/03/10-trends-that-will-reshape-the-music-industry/

10 Ways The Music Industry Will Change In 10 Years

https://www.vibe.com/photos/10-ways-music-industry-changes-10-years

Best Music Making Software for beginners – best DAW 2020

https://www.learnhowtoproducemusic.com/blog-how-to-start-music-production/best-music-making-software-for-beginners-music-production-daw

12 steps to recording a song

https://www.adorama.com/alc/12-steps-to-recording-a-song

The music production process

https://www.music-production-guide.com/editing-music.html

What does a music producer do?

https://www.careerexplorer.com/careers/music-producer/

Create the best home recording studio 2020

https://www.musicgateway.com/blog/how-to/create-best-home-recording-studio

Starting Electronic Music Production on a Budget

https://www.edmprod.com/music-production-budget/

How To Choose a DAW (Digital Audio Workstation) To Produce Music

https://www.audiomentor.com/audioproduction/how-to-choose-a-daw

Music production 101: the 4 steps to recording a song

https://ehomerecordingstudio.com/how-to-record-a-song/

Buyer's Guide: Audio Plugins

https://vintageking.com/blog/2019/07/buyers-guide-audio-plugins/

The Only 7 Types of Mixing Plugins You'll Ever Need

https://theproaudiofiles.com/7-types-of-mixing-plugins/

Virtual studio technology

https://en.wikipedia.org/wiki/Virtual_Studio_Technology

Audio effects, mixing and mastering by Metin Bektas

Audio engineering 101, Beginners guide to Music production by Timothy A. Dittmar

Understanding basic Music Theory by Russell Jones.

Music secrets for the small studio by Mike Senior

Music Production, 2020 Edition

The Advanced Guide on How to Produce for Music Producers (Music Business, Electronic Dance Music, EDM, Producing Music)

By Tommy Swindali

Table of Contents

Introduction

Everyone strives to be an authority or an expert in any or every one of their chosen careers or endeavors as the case may be. For this reason, nobody should be criticized but rather encouraged to be the best or one of the best in all their pursuits.

This scenario is not different in the music production scene. As a beginner strives to become a pro, a pro also strives to either retain that status or work harder to improve until he/she attains expert status. Before we delve into the intricacies of what it takes to excel in the music industry like a pro, we must establish exactly what professional music production entails.

What Does Professional Music Production Entail?

Professional music production encompasses all the aspects, tangible and intangible tools needed to make great and hit worthy music. A pro music producer is tasked with either doing all the work or employing the services of professionals to do it while making sure a kind of synergy is established to produce the best results. Let us run through the various aspects of music production;

• The studio establishment aspects: getting a studio space, which may be at home or a rented space downtown, filling the space with the best budget-friendly equipment available, arranging the pieces of equipment in a way that will facilitate the optimal recording of songs, getting the best software, plug-ins and the likes.

- The creative aspects; talent hunt (budding music talents), music composition, songwriting, creating great music content, or employing the services of great music content creators.

- The engineering aspects; audio editing, analyzing sound recording, mixing, mastering, and exporting.

- The entrepreneurial aspects; publishing the recorded songs, marketing, and eventually selling the tracks to make a profit. This aspect also encompasses the legal and budgetary aspects of music production.

As a professional or aspiring professional music producer, your hands must be in all the cookie jars. This means that you must have an iota of knowledge about the above-outlined music production aspects. The fact that music production is a gradual process means you cannot be a jack of all trade just like that. This is where you have to precisely clarify what you want to achieve with your music production journey. A lot of people go into music production for various reasons; some go into it purely for the love of music, to make money, for fame and popularity, while others produce music just for fun. Regardless of your reasons, attaining pro status is not a child's play. It takes a lot of hard work, dedication, talent, creativity, and the ability to employ a few tricks (the tested and trusted by seasoned professionals).

Furthermore, professional music production entails recording a plethora of music types/styles for different purposes. It ranges from classical, jazz, hip pop, rock, country, pop to movie soundtracks, remixing, etc.

In the professional music and sound production scene, the major operational weapon is creativity and dedication. It is creativity and the ability to polish and fine-tune that differentiates an amateur music producer from a professional one. There is a need to go the extra mile with regards to equipment type, software type, studio space, studio time, and all other tools to achieve pro status.

Objectives of the Book

The moment you have clarified and affirmed your music production end game, you need to work on maneuvering around present obstacles or downright eradicating them so you can achieve your goal as a pro music producer. One fact you should have at the back of your mind is that, if there is no synergy between your chosen music production strategy/technique and your music production end game, your career will be like a feather in a tornado.

One of the major obstacles faced by aspiring pro music producers in the rapidly and continually changing technology and applicable techniques. Another trending obstacle is the unwillingness to delegate the most technical aspects to the professionals. In this game, trying to be a jack of all trade will only lead to a substandard result, which is not your aim, right? For instance, the audio/sound engineering aspects require a lot of skill and experience, which you may not have at that time. What a professional does is to delegate, then supervise and push until you get that clean, clear, and rich sound you want.

Furthermore, we are in the digital era, the fast era. Making that killer music will definitely take a lot of time, patience, and dedication, which very few people have these days. At the end of the day, most upcoming independent music producers commence work on producing a track but end up giving up or not concluding well when things do not go their way, or the whole process starts to seem too slow. This is also an obstacle, albeit created by music producers' lack of discipline and commitment.

Therefore, the book seeks to teach you how to utilize your creativity and inborn talent in conjunction with textbook music production strategies and producer proven techniques in order to produce kick-ass music. Furthermore, the book promises to outline the best available software, music studio props, and equipment that are budget-friendly and, at the same time, facilitate efficiency. The main goal here is to show you how you can ramp up your skill level as much as possible so that you can make a place for your music in today's global music industry with emphasis on 2020 and beyond, help you make great mixes that sound cleaner and richer (marketable), and at the end of the day make great music.

Additionally, you will be provided with music production techniques that have been proven and vouched for by trending and reining authorities in pro music production with relevance to 2019 and the 2020s. Let us have a look at a number of these personalities that have made a name for themselves and their work in the music industry;

Robin Wesley; is a modern beatmaker whose career kick-started from simply having fun with a variety of music recording equipment and then posting it online. As a result of the popularity and feedback, he decided to make a career and ultimately money out of it by selling his beats to musicians, songwriters, and even record labels based on a concept known as beat licensing. Wesley was and is a staunch advocate of establishing synergy between music-making and music marketing (selling your work, investing in your effort) by giving both aspects an equal amount of hard work and focus.

YoungKio; is a 19-year-old young producer (beatmaker) of Dutch origins. He made major headway in his music production career when Lil X Nas used his beat to produce the musical marvel of 2019; ♫old town road♫.

Daniel Jimenez; started his journey right from his university days when he was inspired by Kendrick Lamar's album titled "DAMN." He is a staunch advocate of the saying, "practice makes perfect." He spent a lot of hours perfecting his craft by employing Anders Ericsson's deliberate practice technique, which paid off. The only area he fell short was not being able to achieve the same level of success he achieved in music-making in music marketing, which is very crucial and very relevant if you aim to succeed as a professional music producer in 2020.

The above mentioned successful professional music producers are just a few, among others. Their methods worked for them and made it possible for them to achieve success. No matter if you are a teacher, a student, or a freelancer, this book promises to provide you with ways to breathe lasting and marketable life to your music production ideas.

Yes, this book has promised to equip you with the weapons you need to be one of the best pro music producers; however, the book is not the holy grail of professional music production and therefore does not promise to encompass every and all the nitty-gritty of the subject. It is at this point, your willingness to exploit the web and other learning avenues traditional or otherwise (e.g., EDM podcast) will serve as a great benefit to you in your professional music production journey.

Chapter One: The Professional Recording Studio

The consensus that before you can produce music professionally, you have to either buy studio time at a commercial recording studio or you cough out money which you may not have to open a professional music recording studio is no more tenable. Technology in the music industry and the current climate has advanced to such an extent that such a belief has been rendered mute. Basically, the caliber of sounds you produce does not depend majorly on the location or size of your studio anymore, what counts are your pieces of equipment, creativity, skills, and how you employ them to get the best. Without further ado, let us establish the various types of studios capable of producing professional-level sounds;

☐ Commercial recording studio

☐ Project recording studio

☐ Semi-pro recording studio

☐ Pro recording studio

☐ Home recording studio

Commercial recording studio

What makes commercial recording studios stand out is that they are set up in a way that accommodates various music styles and tastes to satisfy different potential clients, especially musicians.

For this reason, most commercial recording studios have large spaces with one or two much smaller carved out inner rooms for private sound recording and listening purposes. These carved out intimate control rooms allow for simultaneous recordings of different sounds that do not overlap or distort each other. How is this possible? These rooms are padded, paneled, and boarded with acoustic panels, soft wallboards, etc., so that sounds produced inside do not seep out, and at the same time, sounds produced outside do not filter in.

Even though commercial recording studios are structured in such a way that they are able to cater for the music needs of the general public (a plethora of different music personalities), they also vary based on a budget of the owners, the taste of the owners, and the target clientele.

An additional advantage of commercial recording studios is that it allows and caters to post music production activities such as music videos, movies, and TV conjunctions.

Even with all the edge promised by a commercial recording studio, they have become obsolete in recent times because of technological advancement. Technology has made it possible and quite easy to incorporate all the special attributes accrued to a commercial studio to a home recording studio space.

Project Recording Studio

A project recording studio is like a general-purpose recording studio. It encompasses attributes of both commercial studios and home studios. Project studios' similarities with home studios can be attributed to the design, which gives it a homey feel. Project studios are constructed mostly for catering to the personal music recording goals of musicians, engineers, or music producers; however, it could easily be converted to a simple commercial facility, especially the ones not located at the home of the owner. Project studios are equipped with the most sophisticated audio production systems and studio equipment (drum machines, DAW, synthesizers, computers, samplers, synth modules, acoustics and a number of sequencing packages) that are capable of creating a plethora of unique sounds while simultaneously handling other music production undertakings such as audio editing, mixing, and mastering.

In the past, project recording studio cost a fortune to establish; however, with technological advancement and healthy competition in the music industry, they have now become very affordable and easily accessible to everyone, especially upcoming artists. In fact, it is safe to say that all home studios of the last decade exhibit the full capabilities of project studios.

Semi-Pro Recording Studio

The characteristics of a semi-pro recording studio are synonymous with that of project recording studios and home recording studios (a cluster of rooms that are close together or jointed), in addition to the fact that it is structured and equipped with the necessary gear to accommodate numerous musicians recording tracks at the same time. Therefore, the semi-pro recording studio is highly recommended for musicians, engineers, and music producers who have future collaborations in the works.

Pro Recording Studio

When you hear the words "pro recording studio," what comes to mind? A sizable structure dedicated solely to music recording with quite a number of rooms and several professionals running it right? Well, that is not all it is, it is so much more. As a result of the current speed of technological advancements and the promise of even more improvements in the future, you can as well make professional-level sounds in your home recording studio.

Furthermore, there are now online based professional recording studios that you could opt for. Although they cost a lot, many of them may not get the job done to your preferred standard, but some actually get very close.

Home Recording Studio

As stated earlier, it not the size of the studio space or the "state of the art equipment" that dictates the quality of the music produced, although they also play major roles, the music production strategies/techniques adopted, productive time spent, and creativity of the artists, engineers, and other professional staff members are the main determinants.

While a commercial studio is a jack of all trade, a home recording studio is a jack of one trade. This means that home recording studio structures are direct reflections of the owners' music production end game (goals). Furthermore, these goals are determined by the following factors;

▪ Music taste; jazz, rock, hip-hop, orchestral, classical, etc.

- Skillset; a musician or music artist, audio engineering, and inborn talent.

- Budget.

- Short term and long-term goals.

- Willingness to collaborate with other musicians, engineers, and music producers.

As you must already know, attaining pro status in any field is not a cheap endeavor. It costs a lot of money. Money is one of the greatest obstacles afflicting budding musicians and the newbies in the music industry. Therefore, a professional or commercial recording studio seems like a farfetched/near impossible feat for a lot of upcoming musicians. At this point, what is left to be done is to touch up your home studio so that it is capable of producing professional-level sounds if you already have one. This can be achieved by upgrading your gear, software, plug-ins from beginner level music studio props to professional level props. Therefore, instead of continually pouring your limited cash into renting pro studio time, you can build your own custom-made pro home studio from scratch. It will serve as your first investment in your work and the first step you take in monetizing your craft, just as Wesley recommended.

Apart from the monetary benefits, there are other advantages that stem from working from home. Some of them include:

● You are the dictator of your studio time; Renting studio time in a commercial pro studio means you have to abide strictly by the opening and closing hours of the studio. For instance, if you suddenly get inspired, or an idea comes to you at midnight or any other odd hour, you would not be able to immediately work on it while it is still fresh because the studio is not available. However, if you had your own home studio, you would have the freedom to work on your music 24 hours a day if you like.

• A home studio presents you with the freedom to dictate what your workspace should look like. How a studio is decorated, such as paintings on the wall, the color of the walls, type of flowers, etc. may not seem important in the whole scheme of things; however, it helps to provide a tranquil and inspiring atmosphere. This is necessary for increased creativity and ultimately vital for making professional level sounds.

• Psychologically speaking, recording your music personally is highly recommended. It is said to help you build your confidence and grow into your music; then ultimately, you will be able to create and then hone your own unique sounds.

• Having a home studio makes it easier for you to carry out the regular purposeful practice. It makes available the ideal platform to set goals and makes it as easy as possible to achieve those goals.

Reforming the Generic Home Studio into a Professional Music Capable Home Studio

In the first book of the series, which was especially for beginner and amateur music producers, what makes up a result-oriented home studio was explicitly outlined and explained. A lot of emphases were made on software and pieces of equipment that give the best result while being budget-friendly. The approach adopted was a sort of minimalist but effective approach. However, to be able to produce professionally, the minimalist approach is not an option. You have to go all out as much as your skill level, commitment level, and financial level allow.

In the generic home studio as clarified in book one, here are the components required;

– Computer; a laptop, a tab or a desktop

– Sound monitors; at least 2

– Headphones

– A Digital Audio Workstation (DAW) Software

– Microphones

– Audio interface/Sound card

– Optional studio props; Music instruments Digital interface (MIDI for short) keyboard, studio monitor stands, cables, Mic stands, and pop filters.

The above listed have been taken apart and explained with attention to detail in book one. Now for the professional music capable home studio, the following components are absolutely necessary. As we go deeper into the book, you will be well acquainted with the reasons why they are dubbed absolutely necessary, and the ideal quantity, quality, and specifications required. Therefore, the components for a professional home studio are made up of the items listed above and the following;

– Desktop workstation

– Studio chairs

– Both internal and third-party effect plug-ins

– Digital converters

– Bass traps

– Acoustic panels

– Acoustic diffusers

– Headphone amps

Note that all the equipment dubbed optional in book one such as mic stands, pop filters, monitor stands, etc. now become essential for that clean, clear, and rich professional level sound.

Essential Human Components of a Pro Recording Studio

What makes a pro studio a pro studio are the actors, both human and non-human, and the capabilities of the actors. Most of the time, the emphasis is made mostly on the non-human component, but the human components are also very vital. In fact, they are more vital because, without skilled human components, the non-human ones become redundant as the case may be. Let us go through these actors and their roles in a professional recording studio

The Artist: The artist is the total package. He could be the songwriter or the lyricist or the musician. The artist is the component responsible for the level of creativity of the body of the song/track.

In a generic home studio, the common status quo is that one person (the owner) performs the functions of the songwriter, composer, lyricist, and musician. On the other hand, in a professional setting, several artists have to work together. The implication of this is that each activity is delegated to its corresponding professionals. In all settings, delegation facilitates efficiency and great outcomes.

For a professional music capable home studio, having all the actors present is almost an impossible feat. Therefore, what you can do is tap into the available music producer platforms on the web to get in touch with the creative personalities available there. Establish a link, maintain it, allow it to flourish, and you will get a double package deal. How? First, you are able to rub minds with talented people who will help you to improve as an artist. Secondly, you might be able to get your work done for free or at a very affordable rate.

The Musicians and Arrangers: if you want to be able to produce professionally in a home studio, collaboration must be part of your goals. If not short term, it must definitely be one of the long-term goals. To be frank, you cannot do it all by yourself. Being a loner will just not cut it because even those who have been years in the game and have all the experience need outside input, if not all the time, then occasionally.

Musicians are responsible for amalgamating the collective efforts of artists into a single to be reckoned with. Arrangers, on the other hand, are the ones armed with great knowledge of music theory. They are responsible for the placement of the notes, chords, scales, and keys, making sure the building blocks of the song are well placed within the whole song.

The Producer: The producer is the cool-headed persona in the studio. The producer is responsible for weathering any eventualities that occur and also making sure the overall process runs smoothly. In addition to making sure that the music production end game is achievable, the producer is also in charge of monetizing the end product. These monetization envelopes; meeting clients, sourcing for investors, etc.

Composers, songwriters or artists, in general, tend to get emotional and short-tempered when it comes to some aspects of their work. This may cause them to make decisions that may not conform to the artistic or commercial end game of the music. For this reason, the cool-headed and calculating persona of a good producer is crucial to mediate the situation. Therefore, there must be a modicum of trust and respect between the artist/musician and the producer, because their relationship in a recording studio is synonymous with the relationship between a roof and the pillar holding it up.

In some cases, the place of the producer and the audio engineer in the studio may become indistinct because they fit well into each other's shoes. The most common scenario in professional music capable home studios, the producer, the engineer, and sometimes the artist is just one person.

The Engineer: The engineer, as a human component of the music studio, is a highly technologically versed artist whose workload revolves around all that goes on in the control room. In a home studio, it is advisable for the engineer or the influence of the engineer to always be present at all stages of production. The reason for this is that a studio engineer is well informed in all the technological approaches that produce the best sounds possible. For instance, it is important for the engineer to be present during a recording session because he has the knowledge of how the microphones, the studio monitors, and other studio pieces of equipment are to be strategically placed for the optimum result. Furthermore, audio editing, overdubbing, mixing, mastering, sound importation, sound exportation, and even remixing are all within the work description of the engineer. The engineer's role in the studio does not cease at just tweaking, adjusting, and molding sounds into great masterpieces. The engineer also makes sure all the pieces of equipment (software and hardware) are in top-notch conditions so as to avoid disappointments and waste of time when they are needed.

The Assistant Engineer: The assistant engineer is basically an intern in the studio. He or she majorly assists the engineer in executing his or her duties. The longer he works as a protégé under the engineer, the better he becomes until he also becomes an authority too. If you are a novice and you are still struggling with the whole audio engineering shebang, serving as an assistant engineer in a well-established record label or under a well-known successful engineer, will get you far. You can then apply the knowledge gained in your own home studio so you can reform it into a professional music capable one.

The Disc Jockey (DJ) and Video Jockey (VJ): The DJ is technically the marketer and the salesman charged with getting the finished music product to the general public. This is achieved via airwaves and the web, which is the most tenable and popular now. The VJ, in conjunction with the studio engineer, is charged with integrating images, videos, and the likes to the produced song. Music videos (good ones) complement the music, making it easily marketable and sellable, especially on the web. Music videos make songs more realistic and relatable, especially those that exhibit the exact message in the song.

Examine all that has been outlined above. Now ask yourself if it is feasible for one individual to efficiently fit into all the roles and efficiently carry out all the duties attached to those roles in order to produce professional-level music. The consensus is no and yes, which brings us to the next subtopic.

Working with Others

The process of producing great music is an arduous one. It requires a lot of skills and technical know-how as the current climate of the music production scene dictates. It is extremely rare for one individual to have all the skills mastered. This is because these skills are very different, although some are dependent on the others; they require not just practice, online courses, and tutorials but also an experience that can only be gained by working with other actors in the community. Now, these actors might be your contemporaries or your seniors; the important thing is that you have someone or some people to run your work by, to give you a different opinion, and a fresh point of view. This might not seem so important; however, it is necessary if you want to produce songs that sound professional.

In the music scene, what does working with others entail exactly? It merely entails collaboration. Collaboration simply means two or more entities are working together to achieve a common goal. In the music industry, we have collaborations among musicians, artists, producers, engineers, DJs. Collaborations occur between actors of the same skill set (i.e., two or more musicians or producers, or engineers) and actors of varying skill sets (i.e., a musician and several engineers or a composer and a producer). One of the most important tools utilized by professional music producers is collaboration. It is quite a rewarding exercise if established in the right way.

Types of Collaboration

In-person collaboration, as the name suggests, means that each party is physically present throughout the collaboration process. It is the fastest and most efficient method of collaboration.

Remote collaboration, as the name also suggests, means that each party is not physically present throughout the collaboration process. The particular benefit this method affords you is able to work with different people from different parts of the world. It is a slow method, but it gives you more dynamic options that will positively impact the overall creativity and uniqueness of your music.

The current trend in music has blurred the distinction between the two types of collaboration. How? The major cause is technological advancement. A case study will explain better how technological advancement has blurred the lines. Assuming there are three collaborating parties; a songwriter, a beatmaker, and a music producer. Do they all have to be physically present to achieve in-person collaboration? The answer is no because they all could be in remote places from each other (i.e., in different studios across the country or even outside the country) and still be physically communicating through video calls, Skype, and all other related internet platforms.

Collaboration works for professional production. A home studio is technically a solo set. Many home studio owners prefer working alone, but if you want to transcend from a generic home studio into a professional one, then collaboration is a tool that cannot be taken lightly. Therefore, if you are the owner or you aspire to be the owner of a professional music capable home studio, it must be at the top of both your short-term goal and long-term goal lists. Let us take a look at the benefits to your music that stem from collaborations.

Advantages of Collaboration

Ascending Creativity

It is rare for two different personalities to assess a situation in the exact same manner. Each assessment may either complement one another or contrast one another. Now, a contrasting situation may either yield positive or negative results. Therefore, in the positive light, music production collaborations culminate into an increase in the level of creativity and ultimately hit songs. Creative ideas from the participants of the collaboration are examined, fine-tuned, and refurbished into the best it can be. The final idea is then utilized in the production process.

Platform to Build your Career

During a collaboration exercise, each participant has the opportunity to market his or her work to a new set of prospective clients and audiences. For instance, the collaboration between Lil X Nas (hip pop), Billy Ray Cyrus (country singer), and YoungKio (beatmaker) facilitated a geometric-like growth in the careers of each participant. YoungKio got discovered and was signed on by a reputable record label; Lil X Nas and Billy become more popular with fans of their respective genres and also fans of the other party's genre. In simple terms, Lil Nas gained country music fans to his fan base while Billy gained hip-pop fans to his fan base.

Opportunity to Compensate for your Weaknesses and Amplify your Strengths

Every single person has weaknesses and strengths. It is now left to you to recognize them and find a way to balance them. In collaborations, one party's strength might be the others' weaknesses and vice versa. If you are the type who prefers to go solo at all times, then you won't get the opportunity to make use of your collaboration partner's strengths to reconcile your weaknesses. Collaborations also serve as check and balance, a way for you to be accountable so that you don't lax, and your commitment is intact.

Exposure to New Techniques

In life, everyone goes through one experience or the other that teaches them one lesson or the other. Collaborations allow you to learn from both your mates and those that know more than you do as per music production skills.

Effortless Delegation

Delegation of music recording tasks in the studio to the corresponding professionals facilitate work efficiency.

Collaborations are a form of delegation. They make available a platform that allows every participant to concentrate on what they know best and excel in it.

Chapter Two: Studio Design

At the beginner level of music production, not much emphasis was made on the studio design as a factor that significantly influences the quality of sound produced. Now that you are going pro, you need to pay more attention to details and not overlook any aspect of establishing the ideal studio. Why is studio design crucial to your end game? This is because the design of your studio informs the entry and exit of sound, the entry and exit of air and humidity into and from the studio, respectively, and the acoustics of the studio. Designing the ideal professional home studio is a painstaking process. It is an endeavor that requires a lot of time and more money than a beginner might want to spend on designing a generic home studio.

First Step: Find a Professional Who Would be Involved from the Onset

This professional could be a seasoned record producer or a professional studio architect that will provide guidance, which will make your journey faster and smoother.

Second Step: Select the Best Room or Rooms (Two or More)

The following series of advice and recommendations are based on the assumption that you are either aspiring to set up the studio at home or renting space outside your home. As a former beginner who is confident in his or her ability to be able to make professional-level music, it seems more logical for you to upgrade and renovate your already set up studio. Note that upgrading may also mean expanding it from just one room to two or more if you can afford it.

You must consider the following factors when selecting your studio space:

Size: your decision here is entirely dependent on what you have in terms of space and your budget. If you are not sure of the required size, then it is recommended that you get the biggest space you can afford because big sized rooms afford you the avenue to

– Cater to more than one musician, artist, an engineer at the same time.

– Have enough space to accommodate more sophisticated music studio props (e.g., drum kit) you subsequently add to your collection.

– Efficiently make clean, clear, and rich tracks.

Proportion: rooms that have straight lines both at the length and breadth create standing waves, which leads to interference (more on it later). What you can do is to bring in some furniture (useful ones) and place them strategically in the room (i.e., not clustered together). This helps to de-regularize the room to reduce the occurrence of standing waves to the barest minimum. In fact, it is much better if you can get a space with natural acoustics and irregular and unparalleled lines.

In addition, avoid spaces with dimensions that are multiples of the other; for instance, 18-foot by 27-foot with a 9-foot ceiling, because they lead to the amplification of reverberating frequencies that further culminates into an acoustic horror story.

Surfaces: In reference to the three major surfaces; the wall, the floor, and the ceiling, there some qualities you have to look out for.

In the case of the wall, avoid walls with full-length windows, mirror walls, and concrete walls. However, in the situation whereby you cannot avoid the don'ts, you have to be ready to carry out a considerable amount of acoustic treatments to reconcile the shortfalls.

For the flooring, the best option is hard wooden flooring although, tiled and concrete floorings also work albeit with additional trimmings to help them along. It is not advisable to lay carpets on the floors, as they only subsume high frequency and not low-frequency sounds which deter the effect of the acoustics, natural or otherwise. They also become worn very quickly as a result of foot traffic, scratches from moving pieces of equipment here and there, and heavy types of equipment. You can go for rugs instead.

Furthermore, if you are going to rent a space in a story building, opt for the ground floor to minimize the disturbance from foot noise.

For the ceiling, a high ceiling is recommended; actually, it is the best bet so that the full effect of any acoustic installation will manifest properly. Furthermore, high ceilings prevent the incidence of comb filtering that results from strong reflections during vocalization in the studio.

Noise: the incidence of noise is a two-way traffic which means that noise generated outside the studio such as rain, car honks, birds, wind, etc. causes disturbances that distorts recordings while noise generated within the studio such as vocals, piano sounds, drum beats, etc. causes disturbances to neighbors and other people not present in the studio. The problem has been established now how do you guide against it?

Make sure to choose a room far from the far eastern, western, northern, and southern parts of your home. It should be the most centralized room in the house to minimize entry and exit of sounds into and from the studio, respectively. If it is to be a rented space, try as much as possible to get one located in an uncongested neighborhood.

After you must have selected the room, make sure there are no cracks, holes, and dents anywhere in the room so that the effort put into selecting a quiet room is not defeated.

Life is not a bed of roses; therefore, do not presume everything will go as planned. In the event you are not able to get a very quiet location as a result of finances or unavailability, then you will have some soundproofing to do. How do you soundproof? It will also be explained later on.

Third Step: Empty Out Selected Room

After you must have acquired the space either in your home or out of it, it is important to remove all unnecessary fixtures. It might be framed paintings, framed pictures, chandeliers, or any other decorative material that might cause vibrations. Unwanted vibrations are most likely to distort your recordings. Emptying the room is highly recommended because it is always better to begin work on a fresh canvas, which is what the cleared room is going to be. Moreover, if you are the type who likes to hang art pieces for one reason or the other (could be for creative inspiration), you can paint the empty room with any color of your choice, and then have a fine artiste draw paintings directly on the wall, that way there will be no vibration incidence, and everyone is happy.

Fourth Step: Installation of Acoustic Treatment

The next course of action after emptying out space/room(s) is to install the acoustic treatment. Acoustic treatment is carried out for two major reasons;

☐ To compensate for any issue that arises as a result of; room proportion, room size, and room location.

☐ To effectuate the ultimate environment necessary for recording clean, clear, and reach sounds.

Now that you are aware that the acoustics in a room also informs the quality of the recordings made in it, it will not do you any good to just go to the market to purchase just any acoustic material thereby wasting your money in the process; you need first to carry out a sound check to know the exact acoustic problem you have so you can then select the best way to treat it. Let us, first of all, go into more detail of the reason you need to carry out a soundcheck. A sound check will allow you to determine before the real recording starts; how the acoustics of the room will affect the sound and how accurate the sound recorded is represented, and in the event of any discrepancy, the steps you will need to take to correct it. For this reason, it is important to have the basic knowledge about the attributes of sound, how sound reacts when introduced to a room, the relationship between sound and the acoustics in a room, and the rudiments of acoustic treatment.

First of all, how do you carry out a soundcheck? The simplest way is to go for a tour of the studio space, making sure to test every spot, corner, or alcove. As you move around, make a sound by clapping your hands and stamping your feet. Listen carefully for the sonar feedback. A clap test will produce flutter echoes (harsh ring-like echoes). The magnitude of the flutter echoes will tell you if you simply need to hang heavy tapestries and place a few couches, or you have to go as far as changing the ceiling and flooring materials and hanging acoustic panels to treat the room acoustics. Of course, your budget will play a big role in determining the extent of your treatments. This method of soundcheck is quite informative; however, it doesn't give the full gist about how sound interacts with the structure of the room. If you require a more in-depth assessment, you can employ the pink noise test. To carry out this test, you will need an audio program capable of playing pink noise, at least two or more (as many as you can spare for the exercise) speakers strategically placed in the room and a frequency range analyzer. Pink noise is made up of all the sound frequencies in the auricular range played at the same volume. Thanks to advancement in technology, you can play pink noise on your smartphone and also analyze the frequency range simultaneously, using the corresponding applications. When you are ready to carry out the test, set the pink noise to play at a fairly loud volume, then move from one part of the room to the other while playing, make sure to note areas that produce flawed or faulty sound frequencies (i.e., the problem areas).

Acoustic Treatment Versus Soundproofing

These two concepts are often mistaken for one another, especially in the novice community; although, they are two different concepts that cater to two different sound problems. Soundproofing is used to control the rate at which sound goes in and out of the studio either by reducing it or completely obliterating it while acoustic treatment is used to control the reflection, absorption, and transmission of sound within the studio space. Despite the differences in the two concepts, they are both required for better sound recordings that reflect professionalism.

Let's Briefly Talk About How You Can Soundproof your Studio Space

If your studio is located in an isolated environment, you might not need soundproofing, especially if it is going to put a great strain on your budget. There are four processes you need to administer in order to soundproof the studio effectively;

1. Decoupling

2. Adding dense mass

3. Damping

4. Filling air gaps

1. Decoupling: this is simply to prevent vibrations produced by each equipment or surface when two or more pieces of equipment or surfaces are in direct contact with each other, from affecting the other. There is a reason why it is recommended for you not to place the studio monitors directly on the floor, directly on the desk or directly on top of each other. This is to prevent the transmission and amplification of vibrations and unnecessary noise, which negatively affects your recordings. Ductile materials such as foams, rubber pads, and the likes are placed between the surfaces to achieve decoupling. For the purpose of soundproofing, this action is applied to the entire studio space.

Techniques

Duplicate the walls, ceiling, and floor. At the end of this, you end up with a room carved out of the original room. For the ceiling and the walls, you can make use of drywall, plasterboards, or sheetrock.

Installing the soundproofing material is where it gets tricky because it has to be installed such that bass vibrations would not penetrate into the room. How do you do that? Frame the original wall/ceiling vertically with a 2x4-inch wooden plank with a gap of 24 inches between each plank. Screw-in the whisper clips that will hold the resilient channels between the frame and the drywall. Install the drywall or any sound absorption material you wish to use. Make sure there is an air gap of half an inch between the drywall and frame, which prevents sound from entering and exiting the studio.

Float the floor. The floor is the strongest and fastest sound/vibration transmission medium; therefore, the sound created by all the pieces of equipment placed on the floor, such as microphone stand, drum kit, etc., will cause unwanted noise disturbances. You can prepare against that by laying thick rugs or mats to cover the entire expanse of the studio floor.

2. **Adding dense mass**: this activity is carried out before decoupling. It entails thickening the walls, so they do not react to sound waves. Concrete walls are mostly already dense and might not need additional mass. On the other hand, walls that are made from light materials will require additional mass. The most popular and easily assessable material for that is sheet block although, the most ideal is any paneling material that contains a fiberglass core. Thick walls either reflect sound or absorb it. They prevent sound from manifesting outside the boundary it is produced.

3. **Damping:** is a soundproofing method that converts kinetic energy produced by sound waves into heat. Damping techniques reinforce the effects of adding dense mass to the wall. Damping takes care of any residual bass vibrations from sound waves both from within and outside the studio space. Bass vibrations are really sneaky, no matter all the soundproofing already is done, they still slip through even the finest hairline cracks on the wall or ceiling to the microphone thereby distorting your recordings. This is why damping is very important, especially if you are going all out to do a thorough job. The green glue, which is one of the generally accepted damping agents, is used to completely seal up the wall and any spaces created as a result of the installment of wall frames and drywall. It is used to attach pieces of drywall to the wall frames and to another drywall. Have it at the back of your mind that if all these efforts do not completely remove the vibrations, it will slow it down so that its impact is greatly minimized.

4. **Filling air gaps**: this is the reconnaissance and double-checking stage. It might seem unnecessary, but the finishing touches done at this stage will crown all your soundproofing effort. Why wouldn't you want to do it? It is not expensive, it doesn't take time, and it is not difficult to do. What you simply need to do is go over all you have already done, fill up any leftover or overlooked air space such as; window seals, holes from the wiring, gaps from the plumbing pipes, gaps between the floor and the door as a result of elevating or floating the floor, and air condition vents. The tools used are foam gaskets, green glue, and door sweeps.

All these soundproofing's might seem a bit much such that you begin to assume there is no more need for acoustic treatment, but you are gravely mistaken. For a professional level gig, you have soundproofed as well as treat acoustic to make that superb sound you aspire to.

The Rudiments of Acoustic Treatment

How Does Sound Move in a Room?

When a sound is introduced into a room, the sound waves travel in two forms. Some parts of the waves travel in a straight line (direct sound) to the receiving point while the other parts are reflected (i.e., they bounce on all the available surfaces in the room) before landing on the final receiving point e.g., microphone. The direct sound does not bounce on any surface or is absorbed by any surface in the room; therefore, it is unadulterated. The reflected sound, on the other hand, is the reason for acoustic treatment. Reflected sounds in spaces that have been built from scratch with the rudiments of acoustic treatment are automatically controlled. It definitely would be fabulous to find a space already designed for acoustics, right? Unfortunately, such spaces are as scarce as they are expensive. Therefore, you have to make do with space you can afford and then treat the space to sound the way you want.

What are the Acoustic Problems Precisely?

It is important to know the composition of the problems in detail so that you will be able to solve them effectively. The problems can be classified into three fundamental categories;

1. **Stationary waves as a result of interference**: stationary waves are just that, static. They are inert sound nodes that appear to be sitting in a spot when they are actually vibrating, albeit in one direction. Try to imagine what must have made droplets of water spill out of a cup when you place in on the table (or any other flat surface) after drinking. Can't you? Ok, I'll explain. Immediately you placed the cup on the surface; there was a vibration generated from the center of the cup, which spread out to reflect against the edges of the cup and then converged back at the center, creating a force that causes the water to spill. This is exactly how standing waves behave in a room. It gets more complicated, the greater the room dimension.

2. **Modal ringing**: this acoustic problem arises when there are little to no absorptive surfaces in the room. It occurs in a resonance chain of reaction. This resonance greatly influences the sound frequency throughout the room, such that the whole room will vibrate at the same frequency as the initially generated sound frequency.

3. **Reverb times**: it encompasses problems of flutter echoes, unprecedented delay (i.e., not sanctioned by the engineer during audio editing and mixing), and maniacal sound reflection and reverberation, which is bad news for your recordings.

Now to the treatment proper! How can you go about solving the problems, especially those explained above? Each problem will require different treatment plans to solve them. However, each treatment falls under at least one of the following treatment plans;

☐ Brass traps

☐ Acoustic Clouds

☐ Diffusers

☐ Acoustic panels

Bass traps: bass traps take care of a great portion of the acoustic problems in a room. Some rooms do not need additional treatments once bass traps have been installed. Bass traps help to absorb medium, bass, and high sound frequencies. Bass traps are majorly installed at the corners, front, and back walls of a room that takes care of the modal ringing and reverb problem. Bass traps can be classified into; mobile and immobile bass traps

An example of an immobile bass trap is the super chunks (model reflection panels made from inflexible fiberglass), while that of a mobile bass trap is known as Gobos (good sound-absorbing capabilities). Gobos are used to isolate a portion of the studio for the purpose of recording vocals.

Super chunks are structured to stack the entirety of the room corners from floor to ceiling. They are also installed on the front and back walls of the studio vertically and horizontally to serve as the ideal reflection surfaces.

It is all good if you can afford to install bass traps at all the corners, the front wall, and the back walls of the room or at least the corners of the wall directly opposite your microphone stand or opposite the studio monitors. However, not everyone can afford it. With the assumption that you can only afford just one bass trap panel, and you can only install it in just one part of the room. The location to place it becomes the only problem that is actually easily solved. The best and most effective place to install the brass trap panel is the exact middle of the front wall. It should be installed in a vertical and horizontal position, and high enough to be parallel to your ears. This will also get the job done.

Acoustic clouds: when you go into some halls, restaurants, and hotel rooms, you will see a cloud-like structure hanging from the ceiling. If you were not previously aware of it, then know that it is not decorative. It is deliberately installed to prevent sound reflection between the floor and the ceiling. Therefore, it is made up of reflective acoustic panels. Unlike the bass traps that perform both reflection and absorption treatments, acoustic clouds only perform sound reflection treatments. Acoustic clouds become more vital in rooms with hardwood floors that have not been soundproofed with floating floors (i.e., rooms not covered with rugs or carpets).

Diffusers: too much of anything is not good. Moderation is the best course to take, regardless of the type of activity you are into. If you are a well to do person, who has the ability to spare no expense on the design of your studio, then good for you, however, too much padding, paneling, covering, etc., will cause your recordings to sound lifeless and too artificial. For this reason, procuring and installing diffusers is a must as it helps to cure any issues that arise from such situations. What problem exactly do diffusers solve, and how are they different from bass traps and acoustic panels?

Absorbers are installed to minimize the great energy produced by some reflections, so they are not strictly focused within or stuck on particular frequencies. Diffusers, on the other hand, do not absorb a portion of the energy like the absorber panels; instead, they take in the whole energy then weaken it by distributing it evenly in different directions. Where is the best place to install the diffusers?

For small rooms, you most likely will not need diffusers. If the studio space is acceptably big, you definitely will need a diffuser. Place them at the front and back walls, preferably between the brass traps or reflection panels. If you can't afford more than one, place it at the front wall or the wall in the direction where the studio monitors will be facing.

There is a plethora of diffuser types (Quadratic, primitive-root, steeped, two-dimensional, and fractal), which may confuse you. The cheapest in the market today is the Quadratic diffusers; if not, you can opt for fractal diffusers. Apart from being affordable, quadratic diffusers are designed in random patterns that look like books of different sizes arranged in a bookshelf erratically. Randomly patterned diffusers are the best because they allow for very effective distribution of sound wave energies.

Going pro in the music-making community is not a cheap business. It actually devours money and time. Notwithstanding, there are always alternatives. They may not measure up to the standard, but they try. In the case of acoustic treatment, not everyone can afford sophisticated absorber panels or reflective panels, or other fancy acoustic panels. What you can do is install household materials that are absorptive such as pillows, couches, blankets, and mattresses. Furthermore, you have got to put in extra work (i.e., acquiring pieces of equipment that can be used to compensate for poor acoustics e.g., dynamic mics instead of the generally accepted condenser mics and reflection filters) during both your recording and mixing sessions.

Fifth Step: Arrange your Gear

You have to know that you cannot just place your equipment, starting from your chair and workstation to the smallest cable, anyhow. You have to do it methodically to get the best of them. A lot more on the subject will be outlined in the subsequent chapters.

Chapter Three: Setting up your Workstation and Record Station

The way your studio looks and how comfortable it is contributing to your output. Arranging your equipment to maximize output is also very important.

For Your Workstation

Get a chair that promises comfort and will not put a strain on your neck and back as a result of sitting at one spot for long periods. A highly mobile chair (that can move around the room) and one that can rotate 360 degrees will be beneficial to you. The advantage derived from this is that you will be able to move around the studio without having to get up multiple times.

Get a work desk that fits the size of your studio, and that has a few pockets capable of housing some small pieces of equipment such as; the audio interface, the MIDI keyboard, and even a mini console. The advantage here is organization and space management.

For Your Recording Station

The arrangement here should be directed by your music recording goals. There are two types of arrangement

One person only arrangement; this arrangement is the status quo in home studios where one person plays the role of a musician, producer, and engineer. The arrangement goes thus: set up your workstation at the center of the room, facing the front wall (can be also be referred to as the north of the room), arrange all other pieces of equipment such that they are in a circle around you. This makes it easy for you to switch between the roles.

Multiple persons arrangement; this arrangement calls for the division of the studio space into two stations. The first station will serve as the mixing and mastering session while the second (innermost) station will serve as the recording booth. Arrange your equipment accordingly. The set back to this arrangement is that there have to be two or more professionals at a time since one person can be at two places at a time.

Combination of the two; this arrangement enables one person to be in the two stations at once. How is this possible? Thanks to the DAW remote, you can be at the recording booth and still get things done on your computer, MIDI controllers, etc. simultaneously without having to bounce from one station to the other like a ping pong ball.

Now that we have established the studio arrangement, you need to know the type and caliber of computers, software, audio interface, and audio plug-ins that will facilitate the production of professional-level tracks.

The Digital Audio Workstation (DAW)

The DAW is the engine that drives the music recording, editing, playback, mixing, and mastering processes. In the past, what was predominant was the console DAW type, it took a lot of studio space, but it was very efficient in producing professional-level songs. In recent times, the software-based DAWs are mostly used such that console

DAW has been literally pushed out of the music production community. The DAW is a package deal comprising of;

– A kick-ass computer system (either Macintosh or Windows) that is strictly compatible with the DAW that will be installed on it.

– A DAW software of your preference that is capable of fulfilling your music needs.

– An audio interface/sound card.

The three outlined above are the primary components of the DAW. Here are the secondary components which are also important;

– Audio plug-ins

– Virtual instruments (VSTs)/MIDI controllers

Before, you select your DAW system; you need to make sure it has the following attributes;

Integration: your DAW system must be able to speak to and be spoken to by digital recording, editing, mixing, and mastering functions within the software package installed on it. The DAW must also be able to connect with external hardware and media export gadgets easily.

Speed and affability: DAWs becomes more natural to operate the more you use it. You can perform many of the functions in half the time it usually took to run.

Automation: unlike the analog system, the DAW affords you the opportunity to redo a session without losing data from previous sessions. Furthermore, every function becomes automatic once it has already been programmed into the system. That is the advantage of digital.

User-friendly: the operations in the DAW system must be straight forward and uncomplicated enough so the user, you, can operate it effortlessly.

Now, to Take Apart the DAW Components One after the Other

The computer system; you must strive to get a computer with the following attributes

Speed: the processor is responsible for this. Get a computer with at least a fourth or fifth-generation Intel i5. If you can lay hands on an i7, that is even better. Know that your computer can never be too fast, therefore try as much as possible to get the fastest you can afford as much as possible

Memory: for a beginner, 8GB RAM is ideal, but you are going pro now, so you need to do better. Try as much as possible not to do lower than 16GB, so there is no room for problems arising later on.

Hard drive: apart from the hard drive that comes with the computer from the manufacturer, you will need an additional or two (if you can afford it) external hard drives. Get a 2TB minimum solid-state drive (SSD) with a 3.1 interface, a spindle speed of at least 7200 3Gg/s RPM, a seek time of at least 20 ms, and a 64MB buffer.

The DAW software: there are a plethora to choose from; those compatible with Macs, those compatible with windows and those compatible with both. After you must have selected your computer, then you need to select the digital audio software that is most compatible with it. Additionally, compatibility with audio plug-ins, your music production goal or end game, and of course, your budget also informs your DAW choice. Let us talk about the three-leading software for 2020.

Ableton Live 10 Suite

☐ It is very compatible with live performances. This indicates that it is ideal for those with DJ and beat-making goals.

☐ It is a multi-track recording machine that records at not less than 32-bit & 192 kHz.

☐ Ableton live a MIDI with 10 virtual instruments and 41 internal audio effects.

☐ It is also packed with about 23 sound libraries with ingenious sounds of a capacity of over 50GB.

☐ It comes with a free trial package, so you can practice as you like.

☐ It is on the expensive side, as it costs about $800 online

FL Studio 20 Producer edition

☐ FL Studio 20 also comes with a free trial package.

☐ It is incorporated with great automation and mixing functions.

☐ It includes about 80 virtual instruments, including plug-in effects. Therefore, you do not need to buy it.

☐ One of FL Studio's edges over other DAWs is that it has the best piano roll.

☐ It is one of the most affordable. It costs about $200 online.

Pro Tools HD 11 Audio Software

☐ This software is the most popular and generally accepted in professional circles.

☐ It is voted best for teachers and students of music production.

☐ Pro Tools includes about 60 virtual instruments and a plethora of sound libraries. Hence, it is superb for mixing and mastering functions

☐ Apart from recording and editing prowess, it is perfect for post-production activities. Therefore, it is one of the best options for VJs.

☐ Pro Tools communicate and integrate exceptionally well with external drives, plug-ins, and other external media gadgets required for import and export.

☐ It is slightly expensive too; it costs about $600 online. Notwithstanding, you need to really consider it because it is truly exceptional.

Other excellent and competing software are; Logic Pro X, PreSonus Studio One 4 Prime, and Reaper, among others.

The Audio interface: this piece of equipment facilitates sounds into your computer and out of it. Therefore, it works with all the equipment that input sounds into your computer, and those that transfer sound out of it into another medium. It connects through USB, XLR, FireWire,

Thunderbolt, and PCI ports. It works hand in hand with your DAW software and computer.

Audio plug-ins: external plug-ins work with the audio interface to connect to the computer and, ultimately, the DAW. The internal ones (i.e., the plug-ins incorporated into the DAW) are synonymous with applications in a smartphone. They are very vital for mixing and mastering functions.

Virtual instruments (VSTs): if you are not part of a band or you work alone, you cannot joke with VSTs. With VSTs, you get access to a plethora of instruments that make it sound like the instruments are physically present in the studio. It is especially vital if your goal is beat making or a career as a DJ.

Chapter Four: Equipment

There are two sides to a coin in music production, equipment representing one side, and talent serving the other. Having the talent or skills to produce good music is sometimes not enough; you also have to have the necessary equipment to match the skills. You are already familiar with some of the essential equipment required to produce music; this chapter will explore each type of equipment, highlight their specifications and discuss the features that make them ideal for certain types of music.

Categories of Equipment that will be Discussed in this Chapter Include

☐ Mixers

☐ Microphones

☐ Speakers

☐ Desks

☐ Subs

1. Mixers

An audio mixer sometimes referred to as mixing console, merges audio signals, processes them, and then routes (send) them out. With different technological innovations and advancements being released day after day, mixing is no longer restricted to just the big equipment placed on a desk in a studio. Now, with the right apps and up to date Android or iOS software, you can mix anywhere with your smartphone.

But for many producers and studio owners who are used to the conventional way of mixing music, nothing does it better than the dedicated knobs present on a hardware mixer. Choosing a mixer for your studio is dependent on these factors:

- Your budget,

- Working style, and

- The type of mixer you prefer.

The types of mixers covered in this chapter include:

☐ Recording /Live sound mixer

☐ DJ mixers

NB: The distinction between live sound and recording mixers isn't so clear because some mixers are capable of performing both functions effectively.

Understanding the Features of your Mixer

The mixer is a very important instrument in music production, and the more familiar you are with it, the easier it is to produce music. You have to know the necessary ports to connect a mixer to the other equipment in the studio. Then you need to get accustomed to the different controls and configurations used to create different kinds of sounds. The glossary below will help you decipher all the features and educate you on how to use them.

Channels

Channels are signal paths. Mixers with large channels allow for more connection and routing. Channels are constructed to accept connections with microphones, amplifiers, signal processors or preamps, and other lower-level and line-level devices. The number of channels and the features they come with differs, depending on the brand of the mixer.

Channel Strip

This is a set of controls that make up each channel. A mixer is made up of numerous channel strips that allow you to route your signals when recording. Understanding how each channel strip works is not that hard; you only need to understand the basic makeup and operations of one to understand the others. The main job of the channel strip is to send signals from an instrument or mic to wherever the signal is needed. The channel strip or its layout varies in mixers, but its universal features are as follows:

Input: This is where you can select the input assigned to a particular channel; selecting this is as simple as choosing from a menu that opens on-screen; also, you can select it from your hardware interface.

Output: This button is used to control the output of your track; it can either be hardware output or that of the internal signal part available on the system.

Automation Mode: This button allows you to make a selection of the different automation modes available. In the digital system, automation means having your channel strip parameters such as mute, volume, panning, send, and insert level adjusted dynamically throughout a song.

Track Group: This option allows you to group your track with others; this is particularly useful when you are trying to create sub-mixes, i.e., a mixed track within a larger one.

Panning Dial: this dial or sliders, in some cases, can be used to pan your track to the left or right of the stereo field.

Panning Display: This allows you to see the panning position of your track, whether it is to the left, right, or center of the stereo field.

Solo and Mute: this button allows you to solo or mute a particular track.

Record Enabled: this function of this button is to enable a track for recording. It flashes red in all the recording systems, computer control surfaces, and digital mixers. The button is usually located on the physical unit and not on the screen.

Volume Fader: this button is for setting volume control for audios in a track.

Volume Meter: it is usually located beside Volume fader; it displays the volume of the track as the music plays.

Track Type: This comes in handy when you have a system that can record and playback audios and MIDI tracks.

Numerical Volume: it displays the volume of your track in decibels.

Track Name: This displays the name of a track to help you identify what is recorded in the track. Track naming is a common feature of many digital mixers. If you decide to change the name of your track, simply click on it and type in a new one.

Input/Output

Input/output usually abbreviated as I/O indicates the number of devices that can be connected to a mixer. Before you can move your signal around within your mixer or carry out the necessary adjustment to it, there is a need to get the signals into your system. This can be done with input jack or trim control. There is no ideal number of inputs and outputs. The number of I/O you need depends on your plans for the mixer. In a situation where live sound mixing is needed, you would have to calculate the number of devices to be connected and get a mixer with enough inputs to accommodate the devices. You would also have to consider the number of speakers for output, but this rarely causes problems.

For studio mixing, it's another calculation entirely. The devices that would be part of the recording process and signal chain have to be accounted for. There are three basic types of input usually located at the back of the mixer

Microphone: The input for the microphone is known as the XLR input, often comes with phantom power as part of its connection; this is essential, especially for the condenser microphone.

Line/instrument: This can also be referred to as a ¼ - inch jack, it accepts line-level signals from a synthesizer and drum machine, it can also release a line-level output from your guitar amp

Hi-Z: is specially developed for the home recordist. An input of this type makes use of a mono ¼-inch (TS) jack that allows you to plug anything that has an electronic pickup straight into your system, giving you the liberty of not passing it through a direct box first.

Trim Control

This is a knob used to regulate the level of input signal entering the mixer. The trim control is usually situated at the top of the front panel of your hardware (SIAB, Digital, and Analog mixer). The instrument plugged in determines the adjustment of the trim control. Distortions are most likely to occur when the trim control is set too high also when set too low; you get a signal too weak to record, it is important to listen carefully as adjustments are being made.

Trim control has indications for line and microphone signals. The line signal is located to the right while the mic signal to the left, to get a clean sound into the mixer slowly turn the knob to the right for mic sources. Trim control can be used to adjust the level of recording; this is done by turning the control knob in an anti-clockwise direction, which in turn activates the internal preamp. This boosts the level of signal coming from the mic. Often times, the internal preamp of a mixer is moderately good; therefore, most professionals prefer to use an external preamp because they sound better or possess a particular sound.

Buses

A bus is best described as an intersection where outputs from multiple channels meet. Each channel in a mixer sends its signal to a particular bus or group of buses. The channel faders feed the master-mix bus, which routes the main output of the mixer to external devices like speakers and recorders. Auxiliary buses connected to channels are fed by the channel's volume controls. The aux buses route signals via their private output jacks.

Groups

Some mixers with large numbers of channels contain functions that allow you to regulate and process multiple channels simultaneously. Groups work like mini-mixers, with all channels being controlled by a fader and sharing a single signal processing and routing path. This way, the output sent to the master bus is more controlled.

Inserts

Inserts allow for external sound processors such as equalizers and compressors to be connected to specific channels. This is usually done after the channel's preamp stage.

Direct Output

This allows the preamplifier output of the mixer to be fed directly to external devices and recording systems.

Cue System

This allows you to listen to the output of specific channels without altering the combined output of the mixer. The cue system's output is fed to a headphone or monitor speaker.

The Difference Between Analog, Digital, and Software Mixers

While Analog mixers have existed since the dawn of recordings and public address systems, it was not until the early 1990s that digital mixers began making their way into the professional audio world. Over time, the capabilities of digital mixers increased, as well as their affordability. Analog and digital mixers are equally capable of producing high-quality sound; digital mixers are just fancier.

With the 21st century came the powerful computer and software-based mixers, some even more powerful than the regular digital and analog mixers.

Analog Mixers

This allows the routing of signals within the Analog domain. It tends to have a set of knobs, faders, and light for each channel. When you need to change from mixing input to mixing recorded sound, you plug and unplug cords or get a mixer that contains twice the amount of channel as your recorder.

Since analog mixing operations are controlled by physical faders, knobs, and switches, making their use more intuitive than digital and software operations. The physical controls also prove to be a major disadvantage as it's impossible to hide an analog mixer's signal and routing. In crowded studios and cramped places, it is easy to detect when the mixer is controlling and processing a signal.

Even with the invention of digital and software mixers, analog mixers still remain popular. This due to their affordability and simplicity. Some commercial studios simply prefer their analog mixers and their sounds. Besides, many engineers are used to the workflow of this analog mixer.

Digital Mixers

This type of mixer was designed to make life easy. Digital mixers perform the same functions and occupy less space than their analog counterparts. Once you know how to operate it, you perform music magic. Routing signals with this mixer can be as simple as pressing a button. You can switch from mixing input to mixing sound without the need to change any cord; all these are done in the digital domain. The probability of unwanted noise is less because there is no cord to mess with your work. Eventually, if there is a noise in the system, it is easier to find and eliminate it.

One of the most significant advantages of digital mixers is its ability to recall and store mixes. In the event that you have a stored programming route outputs and effects, you can mix and produce music without leaving a footprint. With the click of a button, you can have a bunch of effects that can't be detected like the case of analog mixers.

With the extensive capabilities and amazing flexibility possible on digital mixers, there is no wonder as to why it doesn't come cheap. To get a digital mixer, you have to be ready to spend, but you can be confident that your money was well spent.

Software Mixers

In terms of mobility and space, software mixers are unrivaled. They do not occupy actual in your studio;

however, they may hold a lot of virtual space on your system, phone, or whatever device you have it installed in. You will also spend a lot of money purchasing access to the software as the good ones do not come free.

Software mixers can do just about anything digital and analog mixers can do. It offers you the features of a digital mixer but without its knob and faders. If you are looking for the flexibility of a digital mixer without the overwhelming need to touch faders and knobs, then this is the right option for you. It is usually a part of any audio or MIDI production software program and offers a variety of routing choices without the need for cables.

If you do not have much in terms of studio space, you should seriously consider this type of mixer. It may be difficult at first to grasp the mixing techniques, but with proper instructions and determination, you will understand the process.

Live Sound and Recording Mixers

Packages of live sound equipment typically include microphones, main and monitor speakers, a powered mixer, speaker stands, and the cables necessary for connection. It's usually more affordable to purchase the equipment collectively rather than buying them individually.

With the same set of equipment, you will be able to achieve live sound and studio recording.

For DJ Mixing, you will have to get equipment that satisfies unique sets of needs. Not only will you need turntables and CD players, but you will also encounter difficulties trying to use a regular mixer to achieve a DJ mix. It's best to get DJ Mixers that are configured to handle DJ gears and connect with club sound systems.

Factors to Take into Consideration when Purchasing a Mixer

To get a mixer that serves your purpose best, you need to consider the following questions.

Application

– Are you using the mixer to play live, record, or DJ?

– Is the mixer rugged enough to handle the use you have planned for it?

I/O and Channels

– How many microphones do you plan to connect to the mixer?

– Do the microphones have special requirements?

– Do your other forms of input have special requirements?

– Can the mixer satisfy those requirements?

– Buses and Signal Routing

– How many signal paths do you need?

– How flexible is the mixer's signaling path?

Equalizer

– Does the mixer's satisfy your EQ requirements?

Microphones

A microphone is a device that is used to convert sound vibrations present in the air to electronic signals. Microphones are used for different purposes; therefore, there are different types for different uses. Not all mics can be used in the recording studio, and a good microphone is a must-have in any recording studio.

Microphones can be grouped based on their construction, polarity pattern, and size of diaphragm.

Classification of Microphones Based on Construction

Whether the microphone is as cheap as $10 or as expensive as $15,000, their primary function is to convert a sound wave to an electrical signal. Each microphone discussed in this chapter captures sound in its own unique way. Microphones can be classified into five categories based on construction:

☐ Condenser mic

☐ Dynamic mic

☐ Ribbon mic

☐ Boundary mic

☐ USB mic

Condenser mic: Mics in this category are usually well rounded and have a fast response rate because they operate on the electrostatic principle rather than the electromagnetic principle used in the ribbon and condenser mic. They are good at picking up high transient materials such as the initial attack of a drum. The capsule of a condenser mic is made of two plates; a thin moveable diaphragm and a fixed backplate. These two together form the condenser. The mic in this category has a natural sound to it, but be careful not to place them too close to the transient source, doing this makes them bring out a harsh sound.

Dynamic mic: they work on the principle of electromagnetic induction, which is used to generate their output signal, the mic in this category tends to accentuate the middle of the frequency spectrum, and this is due to their thick diaphragms. They are generally made up of a finely wrapped core of wire suspended within a high-level magnetic field that is attached to the diaphragm. When a sound wave hits the diaphragm surface, the attached coil is displaced relative to the proportion of the amplitude and frequency of the wave. Compared to the condenser mic, it takes a longer time to respond to frequency.

Ribbon mic: Mic in this group also uses the principle of electromagnetic induction, but are really slow in responding to an auditory signal. Due to this, they tend to soften the transient of an instrument. They contain a thin diaphragm, unlike their Dynamic counterpart. Their diaphragm is also suspended between two magnets.

Ribbon mic is not that popular because they are fragile and expensive, but they have a unique sound that is rich and smooth.

Boundary mic: They are similar to condenser mic and can capture a wide range of frequencies accurately, but they rely on the reflection of the sound source to a flat surface. This parallel setup allows the mic to pick up sound from the surface on which it is mounted, so when setting up this type of mic, you need to look for a surface that is large enough to reproduce the lowest frequency. Due to the difficulty in finding a flat surface large enough to reproduce its lowest frequency, they are mostly used for instruments and vocals that don't have a low pitch. One of the major advantages of this mic is that it can capture sound from multiple sources and in a reverberant room.

USB mic: These mics are excellent for producers on a low budget. They are not just cheap; they are also effective. With a USB mic, you can record a solo vocalist or an instrument, then connect a headphone or computer to it and listen. The use of long lengths of wire is immediately eliminated. All USB mics come with recording software, and it is particularly easy to connect it with a Digital Audio Workstation (DAW). They are pocket-sized and can be carried everywhere. The fact that they are small does not in any way reduce the quality of sound they produce. In fact, some USB mics allow the user to select the polarity pattern.

Classification of Microphones Based on Polarity Pattern

The polarity pattern refers to different ways by which sound can be captured with a microphone. There are three categories under this classification;

☐ Omnidirectional mic

☐ Cardioid

☐ Bidirectional

Omnidirectional

From the word Omni, we can deduce that it picks up sound in all directions. This type of mic is useful when you want to capture both the source sound and the sound of the room that houses the source. They can't be used for source-miking as they tend to pick too much background sound.

Cardioid

Cardioid picks sound in front of them but not the one coming from the back. This is particularly useful for live bands because the sound they pick can be controlled. There are also two types of cardioid microphones; hyper-cardioid and super-cardioid.

Bidirectional

Bidirectional mic, according to their name, can only pick up sound from the front and back and not in all directions, unlike Omnidirectional. Often times, it is used to record two instruments simultaneously. Bidirectional mics are also known as Figure-8 mics.

Classification Based on the Size of the Diaphragm

Microphones use diaphragms to pick up sounds. The diaphragm, a thin material, vibrates when in contact with vibrations from a sound source. The diaphragm size of a mic affects the sensitivity, internal noise level, and the handling of sound's pressure level. Microphone diaphragms can be classified into three categories, small, medium, and large.

Small diaphragm: Due to their thin cylindrical shape, they are often referred to as pencil mics. They are compact, lightweight, ultra-responsive, and easy to position. Pencil mics are excellent for capturing sounds from musical instruments like acoustic guitars, cymbals, hi-hats, and other sharp transient instruments.

Medium diaphragm: Microphones with this type of diaphragm sometimes combine the features of both large and small diaphragm mics. They are able to produce full and warm sounds like those of large diaphragms and also have the ability to capture high-frequency contents as small diaphragms do.

Large-diaphragm: This type of diaphragm is popularly used in recording studios to record everything from vocals to instruments, room spaces, and various other sounds. Large-diaphragm mics are the leading choice for high-fidelity recording because they can capture sounds in great detail.

3. Studio Monitor/Speakers

Studio monitors have a huge role to play in the recording, mixing, and mastering stage of music production. They look incredibly similar to regular hi-fi speakers and home cinemas. You've probably come across a lot of them in home studios and mistaken them for regular speakers. Despite their looks, they are constructed to behave differently.

Hi-fi speakers and other regular speakers are designed to sound good, no matter the sound going through them. They possess features that allow them to modify sounds to sound good. The exact opposite happens for monitors. Monitors are designed for critical listening, so the music is played raw and without any refinement.

Differences Between Studio Monitors and Regular Speakers

Active/passive: Hi-fi speakers and other home cinemas are passive and receive their power from an assigned standalone amplifier while studio monitors are active.

Power amplifiers: Active speakers usually have more than one power amplifier per unit, unlike passive speakers. The bass, treble, and midrange cones are powered individually in studio monitors making for a more detailed sound.

Sound: Studio monitors give flat and more precise sounds. There is no fine-tuning; hence the sounds played to give you an accurate impression of the mix, so corrections can be made when necessary. Even if the mix contains errors, regular speakers will make it sound good.

From the differences above, it's best you use a studio monitor for your recording, mixing, and mastering. Using regular speakers may lead you to miss some detail in the sound resulting in an imbalanced mix. Studio monitors can also be used as a regular speaker; the fact that it's designed for professional music production does not stop you from using it to watch TV.

Types of Studio Monitor

There are three types of studio speakers:

☐ Near-field

☐ Mid-field

☐ Far-field

Near-field studio monitors: These are small monitors designed to project sound to close distances. They are small enough to be placed or tables or desks beside the listeners. For effective listening, the listener has to stand close to the monitor as the sound waves it releases is not designed for bouncing off walls and ceilings. Near-field monitors have two kinds of the speaker, woofer, and tweeter. Because they are cost-effective and multipurpose, they are mostly used in home-studios.

Mid-field studio monitors: These types of monitors are usually bigger than near-field monitors and are optimized to project sounds in larger rooms. They also have two types of speakers, woofer, and tweeter. However, their woofers have 3-way designs and are significantly bigger than those of near-field monitors. Their larger woofers enable them to project higher quality sounds that fill larger studio rooms, so they don't have to be positioned close to the listener for effectiveness.

Far-field studio monitors: Monitors like these are usually used for live sound recordings in large halls or musical concerts. In the construction of far-field monitors, more priority was placed on volume than acoustics. These stage speakers are loud and are usually used for fun listening as they are not really effective for listening to details. Far-field monitors have three types of speakers, low-range driver, mid-range driver, and tweeter.

4. Desks

The type of studio desk you have in your recording studio can either make life easy for you or difficult. It depends on the arrangement. A well-arranged studio desk boosts workflow by granting you access to the right gear at the right time. A cluttered desk is bound to slow down the production process and also make you develop a headache at the end of the day.

Some producers choose to make their studio desks themselves to enable them to have 100% control over the positioning. Producers that don't have the time or skill to make a desk resort to buying one. The price of a desk may range from about $500 to $6000, depending on the quality, durability, size, and functionality.

Factors to Consider when Buying a Studio Desk

Desk size: The size of your studio dictates the size of the desk you can buy. It would be unreasonable to get a desk that occupies half of your studio space. Before you get a desk, go to your studio and measure the dimensions of the area, you want the desk to occupy. Have the dimensions in mind when you are buying or designing a studio desk.

Gear Capacity: How many gears do you intend to place on the table? What are their dimensions? Do you intend to buy more gears in the future? The questions will help you determine if the table is a fit for the present equipment you have and any future one you plan to add.

Ergonomics and positioning: Choose a desk whose arrangement supports and enhances your workflow. For instance, is the height of the desk proportionate to your height? Will you be able to access your gears easily with the angles of the desk? Is the studio monitor bridge close enough for optimum listening? All these questions are vital and should be considered when getting a desk.

Build materials and design: The quality of materials used to build the desk will affect the price of the desk. It will also affect the aesthetics, durability, and longevity of the desk. Carefully consider the design and build materials, and choose a desk that will serve you for years.

Budget: Quality studio desks don't come cheap. Getting one will sure dig a hole in your budget, so be suitably prepared.

5. Subs

Subwoofers, generally abbreviated as subs, are loudspeakers designed to give out low-pitched audio frequencies, such as bass and sub-bass, that generally have a lower frequency than the type of sound generated by woofers. Subwoofers have a frequency range of about 20-200 Hz. Subwoofers are sometimes called bass speakers.

There are two types of subwoofers- passive and active. Passive subwoofers are powered by external amplifiers, while active subwoofers have built-in amplifiers.

Chapter Five: Professional Roles in Music Production

A lot of people want to get into music production, but they are unsure which part of the industry they fit into. They also don't know how to get from where they are to where they want to be. To advance in the music industry, you have to be aware of the requirements and the necessary steps. Examples of top careers in music production include

☐ Music Producer

☐ Sound Engineer

☐ Composer

☐ DJ, etc.

Music Producer

A music producer composes, records, arranges, and produce songs. Basically, they are involved in all aspects of music production. Like a film director, the music producer gets to decide which artist to record, how the instruments are played, the vocals to be featured in the song, and the location the song is recorded.

All major decisions concerning a song are taken by the music producer; therefore, he must be able to convey his vision of the final song to the other players involved in producing a song. Those players include audio engineer, mixing engineer, mastering engineer, vocalists, and various other technicians.

A music producer also has to be proactive and plan in advance to prevent scheduling conflicts with recording session players. It will not do book an emergency recording session when the backup singers or lead vocalist is unavailable.

The job also requires great communication skills and the ability to understand logistics and budgeting. Generally, the duties of a music producer include the following.

– Responsible for scheduling the studio sessions until all production work is done

– In charge of the acquisition of instruments for production

– Hires the necessary studio players and negotiates their fees

– Monitors the spending and release of funds

– Guide and coach musicians when necessary

– Create quality sounds that fulfill both the producer's and the musician's vision.

– Assist the sound engineers with the mixing and mastering process (in small record labels that are unable to hire a sound engineer, the music producer takes over the duty).

– Makes sure that the entire production process is done within the budget.

The numerous duties listed above are only done by upcoming music producers. You won't have to carry out all these duties when you become a top-shot producer. Then you will have the funds to hire more studio players and experts to lessen your workload.

Educational Requirement of a Music Producer

A bachelor's degree in fine arts, sound engineering, and music production are beneficial but not compulsory for a music producer. An interest in music and passion for creating jams are the key qualities of a music producer. No one is going to reject you because you don't have a degree in music production or music business.

While it is not necessarily important that you have a degree, lack of experience in music production may be a deal-breaker when job-hunting. You can get experience by taking a course in a music school or interning in an established record studio.

Career Advancement

All careers in music production are extremely competitive. Advancements only come after a music producer has established his skill set and can land gigs with prestigious artists. A lot of top-shot producers began at home and got to where they are by generating buzz with a mix made in their home studio.

There is no guaranteed success in the music industry. With the industry fuller than ever, it's going to be extremely difficult to break-in. Some artiste and producers spend years releasing mixes and demos before they get noticed.

Music producers have average annual earnings of $49,000 and a general earning of $25,000 to $1,000,000. The money is good, but before you can start earning good money, you have to make a wave.

Sound Engineer

Sound engineers, also known as audio engineers, play a critical role in the music industry. Have you ever been to a concert and wondered who was responsible for the overall clarity and quality of the music? Well, the sound was controlled by a sound engineer. They are responsible for mixing, reproducing, and manipulating the electronic and equalization effects of sound.

As engineers, they do not necessarily have to stick to music. They are also capable of handling sounds at conferences, theaters, and other events that require sound projection. They control the microphones, adjust sound levels, control output, and with their well-trained ears and knowledge of acoustics, are able to produce quality sound for numerous purposes.

Examples of Projects a Sound Engineer can Undertake

☐ Radio

☐ Film

☐ Computer games

☐ Television

☐ Corporate events

☐ Sporting events

□ Theater

Specializations in Sound Engineering

As you must know by now, there are four separate steps involved in the commercial production of music – recording, mixing, editing, and mastering. Because of this, there are several sound engineers with specializations in different steps. A single sound engineer can handle all four stages, especially when specialized sound engineers can't be hired. Usually, separate sound engineers are only hired for well-funded events and tours.

Specializations Include

System engineers: Sound engineers in this category are in charge of setting up speakers, amps, and complex public address systems for bands.

Monitor sound engineers: These engineers are in charge of the sound produced by stage monitors. When a band member says, "can you lower the volume of my guitar?" the statement is meant for the monitor engineer.

Research and development sound engineers: These are engineers that invent new techniques and equipment to enhance the art of sound engineering.

Wireless microphone sound engineers: They handle the miking and feedback of wireless mics used in sporting events, corporate events, and other types of live events.

Game design sound engineers: Engineers in this category help with the creation and development of theme music for games. They are also responsible for the balance of the other sounds used in games.

Mixing engineers: Responsible for the "mixing and combination" of the different sonic elements of recorded vocals, effects, and instruments into a song/mix. They are responsible for the balance, volume, positioning, and effects of the song. Sometimes their duty is shared with the music producer.

Mastering engineers: These engineers take over from the mix engineers. They work on the mix produced and prepare it for distribution. The mastering engineer corrects any imbalance that escapes the notice of the mix engineer and makes the mix/song ready for listening.

Sound Designer: A sound designer has to search for recorded or live sounds that can be used as effects during music production. Not all sounds for music used are recorded in the studio. The sound designer procures them from their source and cleans the sound for use in the studio.

Some producers or mixers serve as their very own sound designer. However, if they are unable to get the particular sound they need, they hire a sound designer or buy the sound from platforms owned by sound designers.

Educational Requirement of a Sound Engineer

Many universities and music schools offer specific training in sound engineering. To land a job as a sound engineer, you need to get some sort of training and have some years of experience.

Career Advancement

Sound engineers have average annual earnings of $43,660 and a general earning of $ 20,000 to $300,000. The US Bureau of Labor service projected that job opportunities in sound engineering would grow by 8% in the next decade. This is far higher than the 5% projected for other careers in the music industry. The reason for the higher value is because sound engineers can work in industries that are separate from music.

Composer

A composer is a person that creates and organizes the flow of original music used in various parts of the music and film industry. They are responsible for creating sound recordings that convey stories in film, audio, and video games. They also have to tell the stories skillfully so it will not distract the viewer.

Have you ever wondered about the importance of music in movies and video games? Blockbuster movies/series like Fast and Furious and Game of Thrones employed composers to create scores that match the mood of the movie. Not all scores have to contain lyrics; most of them are just combinations of various musical instruments. A perfect example of such a score is The Game of Thrones theme music. It was composed by Ramin Djawadi and had cello as its main instrument. Another score composed by him that was equally popular was the Light of the Seven scores that played at the beginning of show's season 6 season finale. The score was created with piano, cello, and vocals, and it perfectly expressed the tragedy that would later occur in the episode. Some viewers even claimed that the score alerted them that something huge was about to happen. That is the work of a composer to create flawless sounds that are capable of expressing emotions to the listener.

Projects that Require the Skills of a Composer

☐ Movies

☐ Television shows

☐ Orchestra

☐ Commercials

☐ Songs

☐ Plays

☐ Video games, etc.

Songwriter

A songwriter is also a composer, but a composer who writes songs. A songwriter is more focused on the lyrics of the song than the complete combination of vocals, instruments, and effects that make up a song.

Educational Requirement of a Composer

Schooling is vital for composers. It's important for them to understand the basic mechanics of music. A degree from a university or training from a music school will suffice. Apart from education, there is a need to have a natural talent and passion for music.

Career Advancement

The advancement of composers comes with skills and networking. The nature of their work does not allow them to stay on a project for long. Once they are done with a project, they will need to apply for another job. And if they execute their previous project excellently, the employer may hire them again or refer them to a friend.

Composers have flexibility over their pay as they have the opportunity to charge per hour or per contract. Some composers charge as high as $60 per hour and can work as much as a thousand hours on a single project. Their work can be done in a small home studio, but it must be able to record the necessary instruments and sounds.

Mid-level composers earn an average annual salary of $50,000 while beginners in the career start with a yearly salary of about $20,000.

Disc Jockey (DJ)

Disc jockeys, or deejays as they are popularly called, are responsible for the combination of sounds and music we hear at parties or on the radio. They are real-life at the party! Because, if the DJ can't get the crowd to groove with him, the party is sure not going to last for long. A lot of work goes into the production of sound the DJ plays. A good DJ has to know how to mix, master, and edit sounds. Playing and remixing already created songs can get a bit boring after a while; a DJ needs to be able to create his own beats and effects.

Events that hire a DJ

- ☐ Birthday bashes

- ☐ Night parties

- ☐ Bands

- ☐ Dance competitions, etc.

Educational Requirements

There are no school programs or degrees for DJing. Most DJs are self-taught. After a few years of playing around, some DJs do go to music school to learn more, especially those with interest in producing beats for artists.

Career Advancement

The competition for DJs out there is stiff. There are always a couple of upcoming DJs hanging around clubs hoping to get an opportunity to showcase their talents. The early days of DJing are always tough because they only get the chance to play on weekdays, days with a small crowd, while the top-shots get to own the weekend parties. Even then, beginners are not usually paid, but if they are lucky, they may be able to get some free drinks and entry vouchers.

The selling point of most DJs is their personality. Some are skilled enough to incorporate it into their sounds. People that hear such sounds and like it become fans. DJs need a fanbase to advance in their careers. It's the fans that encourage club owners or party planners to hire a particular DJ.

Networking is also very important in DJing. Most DJs get their jobs through referrals and reviews of previous clients or acquaintances. DJs also have to employ the services of bookers and promoters to help them get jobs and manage their schedules.

Once they start getting recognized and are able to get a fan base, the money will start flowing in. Upcoming DJs are paid about $500-1000 per night, and for top shot DJs like DJ Khalid, the sky is the limit.

In general, the average annual earnings a DJ is about $30,000.

Your Career Choice

After reading about the careers listed above, you must have a few questions on your mind. Questions like, "Which career is more related to your interest and passion?", "Can you possibly have two or more of these careers at the same time?" "Can you use the skills you've learned so far with this book series to start or continue one of the careers?" "Where do I start from if I want to start producing music now?"

Which Career is More Related to your Interest and Passion?

This question can only be answered by you. It's quite clear that you are interested in producing music because you are reading this book. But what aspect of music production are you passionate about? Try to download free software to practice. While practicing, you will definitely find the aspect that comes really easy for you. Develop yourself in that aspect and choose a career that revolves around that aspect. For example, if you are talented at controlling the flow of music and brilliantly combining them, you should consider choosing DJing as a career.

Once you can identify your interest and passion in music production, choosing a career won't be so difficult.

Can you Possibly have Two or More of these Careers at the Same Time?

It's possible to have two different careers at the same time, especially when starting in music production. You would have to go back to the beginning and try your hand at different careers, then stick to the one that suits you the most. For example, you can be a DJ, a composer, and a music producer all at the same time. The workload may be discouraging at first, but with the time, you will find the one that gives you the most fulfillment.

Can you use the Skills you've Learned so Far with this Book Series to Start One of the Careers?

Yes! The purpose of this series is to equip with enough technical knowledge to attempt or continue any of the careers. It would be a waste if you completed the books and are unable to attempt anything in music production. So, feel free and pick a career.

Where do I Start from if I want to Start Producing Music Now?

Start from scratch. Get the necessary software and some equipment, if you can afford it, and start practicing. Develop your skills enough to produce a professional mix. When you think you are ready to share your talent with the world, create an Instagram page for your sounds. Or better still, send your mix to DJs or music producers that are friends and ask them to review the sound. The reviews and comments you get from your Instagram page and friends will help you improve on your sound, and when you are good enough, you may get invited to help produce a sound for a project. That's how Robin Wesley did, so you can! The key is starting immediately. Start now and start small, but think big!

Chapter Six: Making a Hit

Truthfully, there is no blueprint for creating a hit record. Thousands of tracks are released daily. But only a few manage to make it to the top. Studying those few fortunate ones lies the clue to producing a hit. This chapter will dissect a popular 2019 hit sounds and help you recognize what you need to add and improve on in your sounds to make it get recognized in 2020. As a music producer or enthusiast, analyzing tracks of popular artists can be an eye-opening exercise.

Structure and Arrangement of Recent Songs

Most of the songs that popped in 2019 followed the same arrangement tactics that have been popular for a while. The arrangement used satisfied our modern need for a "quick fix." For example, the lengths of all the 2019 billboard songs were between 2.30 to 3.30 minutes. The days when people actually sat and listened to songs of about 6 to 7 minutes are long gone. Just as the world is moving fast, so are the songs being played.

A breakdown of activities done within the average length of 3 minutes shows that the intro of the hits last less than 15 seconds and immediately after comes the 1st chorus. A good reason for this is that most listeners decide whether they like a song or not within the first 30 seconds, and if the intro and chorus are not solid enough to attract their attention, they may skip it for another song. Not all hits followed this tactic; some delivered the first verse immediately after the intro. But even with the verse coming first, it was noticed that the producers found a way to incorporate the 1st chorus into the song within the first 60 seconds.

With the intro, chorus, and verse, the songs were able to attract the attention of the listener; however, keeping that attention was another matter entirely. People today have a short and flaky attention span and will need a reason to keep listening. Songs that we're able to change things up after the first minute kept their listeners hooked. The changes were mild with a few additional harmonies, groove changes, and addition/removal of sound effects every four bars. All-in-all, the flow of the song had to be steady and attractive.

Previously, hip-hop hits used to have 16 bar verses and 8 bar hooks/choruses, but now, 12 bar verses and 8 bar choruses are making the waves. In 2020, new trends will rise with people listen to songs with more beats than lyrics.

– The general structure of recent hit songs includes:

– A short intro

– A couple of verse and choruses, and possibly a pre-chorus

– A bridge-like departure session

– A climax featuring the highest amount of energy

– A thrilling outro

Sounds and Moods that will Trend in 2020

Based on the sounds and moods that trended in 2019, analyst speculates that some of the songs that will trend in 2020 will contain

– Pronounced sub-bass instruments

– Bouncy drum grooves

– Slow tempos recorded for a 70bpm feel at 140bpm

– Fast and rolling hi-hats

– Dark melodies

– Minor melodies

Incorporating everything discussed in this chapter into a mix will not give you 100% assurance of a hit. The trends discussed are based on hits already existing. Once in a while, unique beats that are different from the trend are able to make it to the top. When making your music, don't aim to replicate a famous hit song, make the sound yours and give it your personal feel.

The Production Process

To explain the production process explicitly, the stages of production will be split into six stages rather than the four used in previous chapters. The six stages are:

1. Songwriting

2. Arranging

3. Tracking

4. Editing

5. Mixing

6. Mastering

1. Songwriting

This stage involves the combination of musical ideas to form a bigger structure of audible harmony, melody, and rhythm. The lyrics and the music instrument to be used in a song are determined in this stage. The producer or songwriter/composer envisions what he wants the song to sound like and writes it down in a score.

2. Arranging

The arrangement and coordination of the beat are done here. For example, when the melody of a beat is too repetitive, the problem is identified here and rectified. Some producers do skip this stage, despite its importance.

The arrangement is mainly concerned with the timeline of the song. It allows you to see the attractiveness of the intro, the buildup of the lyrics and melody, and the arrangements of the instruments used for the song.

3. Tracking

Some producers refer to this stage as recording. This is where the recording of the various sounds that will be showcased in the song is recorded. The sounds are usually recorded individually to ensure its quality. Every time a track is recorded, it is played in combination with the other tracks to ensure that it is following the right format.

Some people do combine the tracking process with the songwriting process, but to ensure efficiently, it is best done separately.

4. Editing

This is a crucial stage in the music production process. It should not be combined with any other process and should command the full attention of the editor or producer.

The goal of this stage is to make the recorded performance sound as good as possible. Parts that are okay without editing should be marked as no-go-areas, while parts that require attention should be edited appropriately.

5. Mixing

For many, the fun starts here. The song has been written; the parts have been recorded and edited, now is the time to sit back, relax, and transform the raw song into a masterpiece. Mixing is the most interesting and, by far, the hardest part of music production. What happens here determines how far the track goes. Before you can create a hit track, you need to have years of experience from practicing and learning.

A carefully crafted mix will allow the listener to hear all the instruments and vocals recorded clearly without crowding the sounds. Mixers get to choose the instruments that are more pronounced, the sounds that get to play upfront or in the background, and the type of effects that are used. This stage comes with a lot of pressure and complex decision making because it can make or mar the attractiveness of the sound.

A lot of people focus majorly on this aspect and pay little attention to the other parts of music production. That is unwise because every single stage in the production process has a role to play in the final sound produced at the end of the day.

6. Mastering

This is the final stage in music production. Any error missed by the mixing engineer is corrected in this stage. Any final tuning left to be done on the track is completed here. Basically, the proofreading of the sound and effects are done here, before it is published for listening.

More on the production process will be explained in Chapter Seven.

Working with Bands or Working Solo

Whether you are working with a solo artist or working with a band, the entire production process is the same. All artists/band members participate in the songwriting and tracking process. Even if the song is not written by the artists, they have to participate in the songwriting stage to fashion the lyrics according to their vocals and style. Sometimes, they will rewrite it to sound more like them.

The editing, arranging, and tracking processes are managed by the producer, and in situations where the artist or band members are unable to hire a mixing engineer, the producer will take on the role and edit the song until it is ready for the listeners. It is also possible for the artist to get involved in the mixing and mastering process if said artiste has some experience in creating and editing sounds. It will make the tracking process more straightforward because the artist will be able to share the vision of the final song and nail the necessary vocals quickly.

Chapter Seven: Production Technique

The production techniques employed can also determine whether a song would be a hit or not. As it was discussed in the previous chapter, the intro of a song and the arrangement all work together in creating a piece of music that may go on to be a hit. Producing music is synonymous with a painter combining different colors together to create a beautiful masterpiece.

There are so many things involved in creating good music that listeners get addicted to; most times, it is more than just using the trending structure and moods. Here is a tip that will not only help in improving your sound but will also get listeners hooked to your song.

☐ Make use of a good sound source: Using a good sound source will make your life easier. Now the question is, how do you get a good source sound? It starts with your audio sampling. Become your very own sound designer. Scout your sounds and get creative with the sounds you hear in your natural environment. Find rhythm in movements taking place around you. Who knows, it may just be the sound that will boost your career and make you go viral.

NB: Remember to use the noise reduction techniques explained in chapter two while recording your sounds and make sure you record them separately, so no distortion occurs.

Techniques in Music Production

Two major techniques = in music production would be discussed explicitly in this chapter. They are;

☐ Sequencing

☐ Layering

Sequencing

Sequencing in music production is the process of recording, editing, storing, and playing back a MIDI data. A sequencer is a hardware or software that can be used to carry out these functions (sequencing). Sequencer software includes Pro Tools, Digital Performer, and Cubase. Nowadays, not only is a sequencer able to record an audio or MIDI data, but it can also be used to store audio information. This helps you to create complex arrangements, including synthesizing the MIDI track and acoustic track at the same time. Being able to achieve this makes it possible to improve the timbre of the sample and synthesize sound. The signal path followed by the MIDI and audio data is different, and it's crucial that you understand this difference. Audio data reaches the computer through an audio interface, while the MIDI achieves this through the MIDI interface. Most sequencers are designed to work in a way similar to the multi-track tape recorder, but like multi-track recorders, each track can be erased, copied, and re-recorded. Software sequencer is way better than its hardware counterpart due to its speed and flexibility.

Below are the advantages of software sequencer over their hardware counterpart

☐ It has the ability to change notes, one at a time or over a defined range.

☐ Performance timing can be easily adjusted.

☐ Easy adjustment of tempo within a session.

☐ Saving and recalling a file is very easy.

☐ There is an increase in graphics capability.

Well, one important thing to know is that a sequencer does not store sound directly; instead, the MIDI messages the instrument, instructing it as to what note is being played, what channel it's going to pass through, and its velocity.

How a sequencer works

☐ Recording

Whether hardware or software, a sequencer is designed to emulate a traditional multitrack-based environment through a working interface. A set of transport controls allows the movement from one location to another using the standard record, play, fast forward, and rewind command buttons. Besides, after using the record button to select which track you want to record, the next step is to select the MIDI input port (the source), output port (the destination), and the MIDI channel.

Editing

It is one of the most important features of a sequencer. The ability to edit track varies in each sequencer. The main track window of a sequencer on a DAW displays information like track name, track data, and other commands. The best way to understand sequencing is to experiment with your setup. This section will cover some basic techniques employed when you are sequencing your own music.

Basic Editing Techniques

▪ **Transposition**: This is the process of changing the pitch or the entire note of a track. Transposition is very easy to achieve with a sequencer, depending on the type of system you are using. A song can be transposed up, and the pitch downed (lowered). Transposition can be performed on a whole song or just a segment, by calling up the transposed function from the program menu.

▪ **Quantization**: This is the process of correcting timing errors. It allows those timing inaccuracies to be fixed and adjusted to the nearest musical time-division e.g., the quarter, eighth, and sixteenth notes. For instance, when performing a passage that needs all its note to fall exactly on the quarter-note beat, a mistake can easily occur. Once this happens, the problematic passage can be recalculated by the sequencer to such that each note starts and stop on the boundary of the closest division time.

▪ **Slipping time**: This is one of the timing variables. It works by moving a selected range of note either forward or backward in time by a defined number of clock pulses, or it helps to change the timing element in a sequence. It also changes the start time of these notes.

▪ **Humanizing**: This is simply the random alteration of all notes in a selected segment using parameters such as note duration, velocity, and timing. The amount of accidental alteration that occurs can be limited to a percentage range, and the parameters can be individually selected or fine-tuned. This randomization process can help add expression to your track.

• Playback: After composing and saving your sequence to a disk, it is then transmitted through various MIDI port and channel to devices to make music. MIDI exists as an encoded file and not as audio, and this makes it possible to make changes to the sequence at any time. In the studio, it is now a norm for MIDI tracks to be recorded and played back in sync with a DAW, analog, or digital multi-track machine. When there is a need for more playback in production, a process known as synchronization is employed to ensure that this event occurs at the same time. Synchronization can be accomplished in various ways depending on the device used.

• Saving your files: It is very crucial to backup and saves your session files while in production. Saving of files can be done in two ways. The first method requires you to save your files over the course of production periodically. To better achieve this, you can set up a program that will automatically carry out these functions at regular intervals. The second method involves the saving of files at specific points throughout production. For that, you may save your file with specific names that make it possible to easily revert back to the saved point if there is a need for any adjustment.

NB: Always save the original MIDI file. A MIDI file can be converted and saved as standard MIDI format files, which can be exported, imported, and distributed for use. These files can be saved in two formats:

o Type o: All MIDI data within a session are saved as a single MIDI track while the original MIDI channel number is retained.

o **Type 1**: All MIDI data within a session are saved onto separate MIDI tracks that can be easily imported into a sequencer.

Layering

This is the process of stacking several similar sounds with slight differences together, to create a unique sound. It is one of the most critical skills to acquire in music production. Layering is not without its own benefits as it is a smart way of creating a signature sound, rather than using pre-set which is popularly used. However, layering is not just about stacking any sound upon each other; it requires the careful addition of different elements, which are added for a specific reason.

How to Properly Layer a Sound

Before you can layer a song, there are three major characteristics of the sound you must carefully put into consideration. These characteristics are

☐ Frequency or tone

☐ Transients or dynamics

☐ Stereo field

The first two must be carried out in mono; doing this will help you detect whether your layers are experiencing a phase issue.

Frequency/ tone: Different instruments are made up of different frequency ranges; therefore, you need to be careful when layering so that frequency-wise, they are not clashing. The key is selecting the right sound. You can use the spectrum analyzer to check whether each layer is crashing in the frequency spectrum. You can also use the reductive EQ to create space for each layer.

Transients/ dynamics: The dynamic characteristics of a sound can be defined by parameters such as attack, decay, release, and sustain. The layering of sounds with different dynamics gives it a different shape, sustains the tone, and makes it more consistent. Dynamics layering can be time-consuming, so it is often overlooked. If you are presented with a sound containing a fast attack, you may need to layer it with another sound with a long release or slow attack. This will help eradicate transient build-up, at the same time, giving clarity to your sound. The possibility of clipping and distortion is also reduced.

Stereo field: Stereo should be your last consideration. Why? Because it can mask a poorly layered sound, but if you are able to carry out the first two successfully, achieving stereo should be very easy. Sound can only be panned to the left or right of the stereo field, or you can either increase or reduce the stereo width using a stereo-imaging plugin.

Sound Layering Tips

❖ Be prepared to remove or replace sounds that are not working for your layers; in simple words, don't get too attached.

❖ Less is better, minimize as much as possible the number of your layers. This does not imply that you can't stack more than five sounds together, but if there is a layer available that can perform the work of two or more layers, be sure to use it.

❖ Thinner sounds are better for layering.

❖ Make a habit out of re-pitching your sounds, as it helps two or more sound to gel even before the addition of effects.

❖ Be sure to avoid repetition, use different combinations of layers.

Chapter Eight: Recording

The recording is exciting for those already familiar with it, if you've ever been to a recording studio and observed the way a professional works around the instrument, you will admit, it's quite fascinating, his interaction with the mixing board, pushing a button here and there. You can't just start recording with any type of mixer, the choice of your mixer depends on the type of instrument accessible to you in your studio and your budget.

Three Basic Types of Recording Systems

Studio-in-a-box (SIAB) system: this is an all in one unit that comes with a digital mixer, most mixers in this category are quite easy to navigate, you only need to plug in your instrument or your microphone, and you are good to go. This category of mixers is flexible in routing signals, allowing you to achieve much with little to no hassle. Although the mixers in each SIAB system vary in terms of specification and features, so before you get one of these, make sure to check if it has your desired feature.

Computer-based system: All recording software comes with their own digital mixer that is controlled by your keyboard and mouse. This software also allows you to access an external bit of hardware known as Computer Control Surface (CCS), which lets you work with physical knobs and sliders. The CCS can be handy, especially when you decide to use a computer-based Digital Audio Workstation and want to control the virtual mixer with some hardware. While the computer control surface performs the function of a digital mixer, not all computer control surface is compatible with each software, so before you get the computer control software, check to see if it is compatible with your system.

Stand-alone components: In this system, everything is separate. Here, you need to buy a mixer before you can make use of your recorder. But the advantage of this system is that you get to choose between an analog or digital mixer. Also, you get to choose your cords, and as these are essential for the proper connection, it can be quite expensive.

Mixers

The mixer is very important equipment in recording, and the more familiar you are with it, the easier it is for you to produce music. It gives you control over a variety of input and output configurations. Picture your mixer as a traffic controller communicating with different units to make the traffic move faster and avoid a collision. They route all signals, both incoming and outgoing coming from the instrument and recording device and make sure they get to their desired destination without a hitch. Understanding the mixer encompasses the input, trim control, and the channel strip. The moment you are well versed in their functions and how they operate, then operating a mixer becomes an easy feat to achieve.

Understanding Signal Flow in Recording

The movement of signals within your system is one of the essential things to remember when recording. You will appreciate having this knowledge as it helps you to create music exactly as you envisioned it in your head. Here is how a signal moves through your channel strip:

Source Audio or Input: This is the signal coming from your hardware input or record, or the signal recorded on your hard drive. Your signal originates from your audio source and moves to the channel strip.

Insert: This function allows you to insert effects such as equalizer and dynamic processors when there is a need to change the sound of the entire signal.

Send Pre Fader: This function allows you to route part of your signal out to an Aux bus where effect such as reverb can then be inserted. With effects like reverb, you would want to control how much of the effects you can hear since it's only a part of the signal you are dealing with and not the entire portion. To achieve this function, you adjust the knob or slide to send as much or as little of the signal to the right Aux component.

Send Postfader: When your pre button has been disengaged, your track passes through the track fader from where a signal is sent.

Pan: This button allows you to adjust the amount of signal going to the left or right of a channel connected to the stereo output.

Output: This is the destination of your signal as it leaves the track channel strip, it can be a master bus, an aux, or a semi bus (from where it is then directed to the master bus).

Understanding Mixer Routing

Routing or Busing can simply be explained as the process of sending a signal obtained from an instrument connected to the channel strip out to where it can be processed. The first stop of the signal when it is sent out is a bus. There are three types of buses that can receive a signal

☐ Master bus

☐ Aux bus

☐ Submix bus

Master Bus

This is where your song is actually being mixed. From the master bus, you can choose which physical output the signal would be sent to. The pan button on the channel strip allows you to know the amount of signal sent either to the left or right of the stereo field. The master bus has its own dedicated channel strip, which is a stripped-down version of the regular one that allows you to add special effects such as compression and EQ. The master bus channel strip does not have a routing option such as input selection, solo, and mute button. This is because you are in the final stage of your signal flow, so you don't really need them. Remember, the fader in each channel is used to control the level of the signal sent to the master bus and the volume level of each signal; therefore, the master fader is used to determine the overall volume of all channels that are routed to it before it is sent to a desirable output device.

Aux Bus

This is where your signal goes to when one of the send function is being used on the channel strip. Aux bus also has a dedicated channel strip of its own, where you can insert some desirable effects such as reverb. When you are done with the changes you need to make, the next stop of the signal is the master bus. There it can mix with the other signals that make up your track.

Sub-Mix Bus

Sometimes, you may want to control a group of instruments independent of the master fader. To do this, you can create a group for the track and sub-mix them so you can adjust the volume without affecting the other instruments that are not in the group. The process is called Submixing, and the signal is sent to the sub-mix bus. From the sub-mix bus, the signal moves to the master bus, where it is blended with signals coming from other tracks. In the case of software mixers that are not in possession of a sub-mix bus, you can perform this function by simply routing your signal to any internal buses; from there, you can adjust the level using the channel strip fader associated with the internal bus.

Output Jacks

Mixers contain a couple of output jacks that are located at the back of your hardware. There are different types of output jacks in a mixer;

Monitor Jack

The monitor jack has the same signal as that of the master out jack and headphone jack but provides another space where a speaker or headphone can be plugged. It can also be used for Hardware monitoring on systems that have it; this is majorly common with a computer-based audio interface. It enables you to monitor the signal from the audio interface, instead of the signal going to the computer and back out before it reaches your ear – it reduces the latency that is heard when listening to yourself as you record.

Master Out Jack

It goes to the power amp of your speaker or directly to any powered monitors if you have one. It is controlled by the master fader.

Phone Jack

This output jack is solely for your headphone, and it is fed by the phone knob of the master control. It carries the same signal as that of the master bus, but with the phone jack, you can control the volume separately.

Microphones

This often the first device in a recording chain. A mic is a transducer that changes one form of energy to another, and in this case, the sound wave is transformed into an electrical signal. The quality a microphone picks up is often influenced by a number of external variables like the placement, acoustic environment, and distance or dependent on the design, which can be type, characteristics, or quality. The primary function of a microphone is to capture sound, but it can also be used to infuse a particular sound tone into a performance. There is also the preamp that helps boost the signal as it travels through the recorder. The combination of the two can help create a distinct sound or add a certain texture to your sound.

Miking Technique

It has already been established that microphones are important devices in recording, so also is their placement. Some microphones will get you your desired sound when they are placed in a particular way.

There are four types of miking techniques, and each will be discussed in this chapter

1. Spot miking

2. Ambient miking

3. Distant miking

4. Stereo miking

Spot Miking

Spot miking, also known as close miking, involves placing your microphone 1-3 feet within the sound source. This is done because sound diminishes with each square meter; it moves from the sound source. Spot miking creates a tight, present sound, and it is able to exclude the acoustic environment. This technique is mostly favored by home recordists because it adds a little of the room to the recorded sound. A disadvantage of spot miking is that it tends to create a less natural sound, and if you are not careful, it will compromise the quality of your recording.

Factors to Consider when Using Spot Miking

Spot miking picks up more of transient materials, which can make your recording sound harsh. Whenever you are using spot miking for a transient instrument, move the mic back a bit or slightly point it away from the sound source.

Spot miking can be used to isolate many instruments on your track, and this will make your mixing process easier.

Ambient Miking

This technique requires placing the mic at a distance far enough for it to capture the room sound (reverb and delay). The room sound can be equally or more prominent than the direct sound source. The mic is placed a few feet away from the sound source but pointed in the opposite direction to the sound. But in doing this, you cannot capture the attack of the instrument, so to overcome this effect, use a spot mic for the instrument. After recording, blend the sounds from both mics during the mixing process.

Another factor you need to consider is the room, does it have a good sound? If not, you are better off using only the spot-miking technique. The best place to use the ambient miking technique is when the room has a good sound, such that when it is mixed with spot mic, it creates a natural reverb. Also, in a live concert, the ambient mic can be placed over the audience to pick up their reactions.

Distant Miking

This involves placing the mic 3-4 feet away from the sound source. This technique can capture part of the room's sound and that of the instrument as well, creating a tonal balance. Distance miking can be used for an entire instrument ensemble, for example, the drum set. Ambient mic, coupled with a spot mic, will help create a natural sound, but the pickup relies heavily on the acoustic environment. The mic should be placed at a distance that will help create a tonal balance. With the distant technique, your recording can have a live feeling to it, but the downside of this is that if your acoustic environment is not good enough, it reflects in your recording and will result in a muddy sound. To overcome this, you can place your mic closer to the source and add a degree of artificial ambiance.

Stereo Miking

This technique involves the use of two microphones to capture a coherent stereo image. This technique can be applied to distant or spot miking of a single instrument. There are several stereo miking techniques, and they are:

☐ X/Y

☐ Spaced pair

☐ Mid side (M/S)

☐ Decca technique

☐ Blumlein pair

X/Y Pair

The X/Y coincident stereo miking involves placing two mics of the same type, same manufacturer and model next to each other such that their diaphragm is so close without touching each other. The two mics face each other at angles between 90o and 1350, with the mid-point pointing outward towards the sound source. Nowadays, you can easily purchase a microphone with two diaphragms in the same casing. They are designed to allow the top diaphragm to rotate at 1800, allowing for adjustment of X/Y angles, or they can be fixed at angle 900.

Space Pair

This involves placing two mics at a distance range of several feet to 30 feet from the instrument or ensemble. The major disadvantage to this technique is the tendency of phase discrepancy to occur, and when mixed in mono, this phase discrepancies lead to variation in frequency response.

Mid- Side (M/S)

This is another coincident-pair system that is similar to the X/Y technique. The only difference is that it requires the use of a software plug-in, an external transformer, or an active matrix to work. In this technique, one mic, usually a cardioid mic, is designated as M (mid), which faces the sound source while the second mic is a bi-directional mic, designated as S (side). S is positioned perpendicular to M; therefore, M picks up sound directly from the source while S captures ambient and reverberant sound.

Decca Pair

This technique is mainly used for recording classical, orchestra, and large ensembles. It consists of three omnidirectional mics in which two mics are placed three feet apart (one to the right and the other to the left), while the third one is placed about 1.5 feet to the front. The three mics are panned to match their configuration.

Blumlein Pair

This is also similar to the X/Y pattern, but the difference is that the two bi-directional mics are placed at angle 900 to each other with the diaphragm as close as possible. The advantage is that the bi-directional mic is able to pick up sound from the front and back, creating a natural sound.

Mic Placement for Different Instruments

Some mics work better in certain situations than others. This is due to the characteristics of some mic that allows them to be better equipped for a particular instrument. For instance, a condenser mic is better suited for an orchestra, where you want to pick everyone's voice, than a dynamic mic.

Choosing the best mic for your instrument or vocal depends on the type of sound you are aiming for, whether it is Punchy (which your best choice is the dynamic mic), mellow -which ranges from clear to croony, depending on the distance involved (the best choice is ribbon mic).

Vocals

The human voice is a versatile sound source ranging from a shout to a whisper. There are different dynamics and timber in it, but generally, most people prefer a large-diaphragm condenser for vocals. Note that the choice depends on the sound you are aiming for. When you are in need of a dirty or raw sound, or in another case, there is a need for the singer to scream; then a dynamic mic should be your choice of the mic. But if you are aiming for a light sound, then the small diaphragm condenser mic should be your choice. Also, when you are miking for backup, the omnidirectional mic may be your choice as the singer can stand around it.

Acoustic Guitar

It is characterized by a set of rich overtones. Mic placement for an acoustic guitar varies and may require experimentation to get the best type of microphone and placement. For optimum pickup:

The mic can be placed at 6-18 inches away from the guitar, and 3-4 inches below the point where the neck meets the body of the instrument.

You can also place the mic 3 feet away and point it directly to the soundhole; this captures the rich sound coming directly from the soundhole and the string.

Generally, for an acoustic guitar, you need a condenser mic, but if your intention is to get a richer sound, then a ribbon mic is the best choice. Your mic placement can be three inches to a foot or more depending on the type of sound you intend to get.

Also, for a louder instrument, choose a condenser mic or shift the mic away from the particular instrument a bit.

Electric Guitar

Once again, the type of miking depends on the sound you are trying to achieve. If your aim is to get a distorted rock sound for your electric guitar, then a dynamic mic will help you achieve this. A small condenser mic can also help accomplish this feat. Sometimes, the type of mic used does not matter, but the placement of the mic does, and to get the best sound from your guitar amp, the mic has to be placed 2-12 inches from the amp cabinet, with the mic pointing directly to the cone of the amp. For speakers, sometimes a slight shift to the left or right is all it takes to achieve your sound.

After performing the procedure above, if you are still not getting your desired sound, you can add a second mic 3-4 feet away or point the mic directly at the speaker cabinet to produce an ambient sound.

Electric Bass Guitar

Miking an electric bass guitar can be a real thorn in your side as it is very easy for the sound to be muddy and thin at the same time. You might think it is not possible for a sound to lack definition and be thin at the same time, but it does happen. To avoid this, you can run your bass guitar into the board through a direct box, Hi-Z, or an amp line out jack on the mixer; this helps a punchier sound.

Due to their low frequency, a dynamic mic or a large-diaphragm mic is the best option. When setting up the mic, it should be placed at 2-12inches away from its amp speaker, or you can angle the mic and let the speaker sound drift past the mic diaphragm.

Piano

Recording a piano sound can be tough, especially if the acoustics of your room is not so great. Due to the piano's size, you need a large room with high ceilings to record it. When piano sounds, the best type of mic to use is the condenser mic, whether it is a large-diaphragm mic or a small one, but getting your desired sound depends on its placement. If you are aiming for a natural classical sound, your mic should be placed 2-6 feet away from the instrument, depending on the amount of room sound you want in the mix. Remember, the farther away your instrument is to the mic, the more room sound it picks up.

Mic placement for a piano also depends on the type. For example, the grand piano which is an acoustically complex instrument can be miked in different ways depending on your preference, because of its size, a minimum distance of 4-6 feet is required a well-developed tonal balance and full pick-up. Sometimes, this is not feasible due to leakage from other instruments. Usually, when miking a grand piano, a condenser or dynamic mic is the preferred choice, but if there is a problem of excessive leakage from other instruments, then your best option is a closed-mike cardioid. There are several positions where a mic can be placed on the grand piano.

Position 1: a boundary mic is attached to the partially or entirely open lid.

Position 2: two mics are placed at a working distance of 1-6 inches, one is positioned over the low string while the other over the high string, using the stereo spaced pair configuration.

Position 3: a mic is placed inside the piano between the soundboard and the partially open lid.

Position 4: two mics are placed outside the lid in the stereo pair configuration.

Position 5: a single mic is placed over the piano hammer at a working distance of 4-8 inches.

For the upright piano, the miking technique is different from the grand piano since the former is designed for home enjoyment. There are different methods of miking an upright piano.

Method 1: miking over the top

The two mics are placed in a spaced fashion, one over the piano and the other in front of the piano's opened top. You can reduce resonance by angling the piano away from the wall.

Method 2: placing mic over the upper soundboard area

The mic is placed about 8inches from the soundboard, above both the bass and high string. This helps reduce excessive hammer attack.

Drum Set

Getting your drum to sound fantastic depends on the type of sound you want. The first step to getting a good drum sound is proper tuning and a good head. When you invest time in selecting head and proper tuning, you are already halfway to getting a good sound; mic placement only contributes little to achieve this.

Kick drum: When recording a kick drum, the best mic is a dynamic mic. Some dynamic mic is specially designed for the kick drum. The mic can be placed halfway within the drum.

Snare drum: For the snare drum, the best option is a Cardioid pattern mic due to its location to other drums, especially the hi-hats. The mic is placed between the small tom-tom and the hi-hat about 1-2 inches from the snare head. This gives a punchy sound. For a crisper sound, add a second mic under the drum, placed at 1-2 inches from the head with the diaphragm pointing to the snare.

Hi-hat: For the hi-hat, a dynamic mic or a small diaphragm condenser mic is the best option. The dynamic mic gives a trashier sound while the condenser gives a bright sound. Both can be adjusted using EQ; the mic should be placed 3-4 inches above the hi-hat and pointed downwards. For hi-hats, the placement of the mic does not matter unlike that of the other instruments because of the tone, but be careful that your mic is not touching the hi-hat.

Most times, people don't mic the hi-hat because of the sound. But there are a lot of ways to mic the hi-hat. The first one is placing the mic on top of the cymbal; this will pick up the sound, or you can place the mic at the edge of the hi-hat and angle it in a way that is slightly below or slightly above the meeting point of the cymbals.

And if you are in a situation where there is only one mic, you can place it in between the hi-hat and the snare drum, facing it away from the rack tom as much as possible.

Tom-tom: The best mic for the tom-tom is the dynamic mic. For the rack tom (the one mounted above the kick drum), you can use one or two mics. In the case of one mic, place it between the two drums 4-6 inches away from the head, and if there are two mics available, place it 1-3-inches above each drum. The miking of small tom is similar to rack tom.

Miking the entire drum kit: Sometimes, there is a need for an overhead ambiance mic. If for no other reason than to pick up the high-transient sound of the cymbal. The best mic option for this is the ribbon or condenser mic (both large and small diaphragm), but preferably the latter because of its accurate high-end response. Condenser mic can pick up the high cymbal frequency and also give the drum sound at a certain brightness. For overhead miking, you can use one or two mics but preferably two. There are two techniques for overhead miking; they are:

☐ X-Y coincident technique

☐ Stereo pair technique

For the two techniques, the mic should be placed 1-2 feet above the cymbal. The X-Y mic should be placed at the center, just forward of the drummer's head, while for the stereo pair technique, the mics should be placed 3-6 feet apart and then pointed downward, towards the drum set.

Hand drums: the type of mic used, and placement depends on the drum itself and the tonal characteristics. For instance, the conga has a mid-range frequency and produces a large sound. So the best mic option is a condenser mic that can be able to capture the sound. Miking a hand drum also depends on the sound you want, if you are aiming for a tighter and drier sound, you can use a dynamic mic.

For the smaller high-pitch drums, it is preferable to use a condenser mic (both small and large-diaphragm) than a dynamic mic. Generally, for all hand drums, the mic should be placed 1-3 feet from the drum.

Chapter Nine: Mixing

What is mixing? Mixing is the process whereby a multi-track material is blended, treated, and combined into a multi-channel format. The multi-track material can be a record, a sample of the synthesized material. But in the advance sense, it simply means recording and blending tracks together through several processes to make it sound cohesive and balanced. A mix is the sonic representation of creative ideas, performance, and the emotions you are trying to project. A mix can be a factor that will determine the success of your album. The main aim of mixing is to turn a different track into a homogenous mixture.

Characteristics of a Good Mix

• **Balance**: The different frequency bands should be in a balanced proportion with each other. Also, it should have a left-right balance.

• **Clarity**: Even though the aim is for the track to blend together, it is still important for each instrument to be heard. In a good mix, you should be able to identify the kick drum and the bass as a separate part.

• **Emphasis**: The hook of a song should be attractive without having any mastering and mixing tricks.

• **Multi-dimensionality**: A good mix should be able to give the impression that some instruments are placed in the front, while some are placed to the back, left and right.

Listening

Listening is a very important skill to acquire in mixing. It may seem easy, but it is not. You need to develop ways to verify whether the sound you are hearing is truly what you are hearing. Over the years, in order to verify this, a lot of techniques have been developed.

Some of the Techniques Developed are Discussed Below

• **Listen to multiple monitors**: This is very important, especially when you are trying to get the balance of a mix. Even though all your work can be done on a single monitor, it does not hurt to check your mix against other sources as well. Most mixers settle for a set of monitors they feel is right for their music, familiarize themselves with its strengths and weaknesses, while using another smaller set of speakers to check the balance. These monitors do not have to be the best; in fact, if the monitors are terrible, it is an advantage because the majority of the listeners may not have the quality of your own speaker, so you get to hear how they will hear the sound in the real world. These speakers can range from a computer extension speaker to earbuds. The main reason for this is to check whether one instrument is not too loud or too low. Balancing is also one of the main arts of mixing, especially getting the kick drum and the bass guitar to sound well on a smaller monitor.

• **Listening in mono**: Since you will get to listen to your mix in mono, it is better to start as early as possible. Doing this helps a mixer to discern phase coherence, balancing, and even panning.

Processes and Techniques Involved in Mixing

Before you start any mixing process, preparation for mixing is very important. Like the saying, proper preparation prevents poor performance. In mixing, it helps you avoid unnecessary mistakes and make your work easier.

Over the years, preparation for mixing has evolved. Once upon a time, preparing for mixing is about labeling your console and setting up your outboard gears, but today it is much more than that. It involves a series of processes like labeling your file and making your track layout within the DAW. Preparation for your mixing session can be carried out through the following steps:

☐ Make a session file copy

☐ Eliminate noise

☐ Tweak your track timing

☐ Check your fades

☐ Tune your track

☐ Comp your track

☐ Arrange your track

Mechanism of Mixing: The Overall Approach

Most mixers already have an idea of the final version of their mix before they even start mixing, so they take their time to familiarize themselves with the song first. Whether they are aware of it or not, most mixing engineers have their own approach to a mix, although this may vary depending on the song, artist, or genre. Their techniques are basic: determine what they want from the song, the direction, the feeling they want to generate, develop the groove, find the most important element in the mix and emphasize it. All these techniques are innate in most mixers such that they find themselves carrying out these processes without realizing they are following the pattern.

Three-dimensional mixing (tall, wide, and deep) is a characteristic common among great mixers.

The tall signifies frequency; all instruments involved in a mix have to balance frequency wise, i.e., all the frequencies must be properly represented.

The deep signifies the dimension. It is achieved by introducing ambiance elements to the mix through +reverbs, delays, and offshoots like chorusing. But this is not the only factor that gives depth to a mix; other factors include a mic, overheads, rooms, and leakage from other instruments.

The wide signifies panning; placing the audio element in the sound field must be able to create an interesting soundscape where all elements in the mix can be heard more clearly.

Elements of a Mix

There are six main elements to creating a great mix; they are:

• **Balance**: This is of the utmost importance; all the other elements pale in importance. It is the volume-level relationship between musical elements. Before you can create a good balance, your arrangement must be excellent.

A good balance starts with a good arrangement. Arrangement in a mix is about tension, release, and dynamic changes such loud versus quiet, full versus sparse.

- **Dimension**: It involves adding ambiance to a musical element. It can be captured during recording, but creating or enhancing dimensions usually occur during mixing through the addition of effects like reverbs, modulation, and delay. Dimension is used to create an aural space, add excitement or add width and depth to a track.

- **Panorama element**: This is one of the elements of a mix that is commonly taken for granted. It involves placing the audio element in a sound field and understanding this element, and we must familiarize ourselves with the stereo system.

- **Frequency element**: The main tool here is the equalizer. It involves having all the frequency of an element well represented in the mix.

- **Dynamics**: Manipulation of dynamics, such as compression, limiting, plays a major role in sound. It involves the manipulation of the volume envelope of an individual track or the entire mix by increasing the level of soft sound and lowering the high one. This helps to keep the level of the sound in balance.

- **Interest**: this depends on you; it is what is added to make the mix special.

Techniques for Mixing a Solo Project

☐ Know your aim for the mix: mixing starts even before you have an idea of the sound. You should have an idea of the element needed, the frequencies, and so on, even before you begin the mixing session. Also take your time to select sound and samples that will work well together, remember this matters a lot – your goal is for the element to sound well together and not as individual parts.

☐ Make use of Automation: Automation will help accentuate some parts, for example, when you need to slowly filter the bass during a build-up and then bring it back on the drop.

☐ Check your mix at different volume: it is better to mix at a lower volume, but does not to hurt to turn the volume up now and then. We hear different frequencies at different levels, so doing this will give you an overall idea of the sound.

☐ Use a reference track: select a professionally released track and use it to compare your own, remember the reference track will be louder than your own as it has been mastered, so make sure to bring the volume down.

☐ Be careful not to over-compress your mix: Compressing one instrument can make it sound better, but compressing a whole mix can give it a dull, flat sound that tires your ears.

Chapter Ten: Mastering

Before you can fully create a piece of music, it has to go through several processes such as songwriting, recording, mixing, and finally mastering. It is the last step in the finalization of audio recording. In mixing, you work with individual tracks while in mastering, you work with the entire mix. Mastering is a combination of different processes that boil down to three primary processes – equalization, compression, and limiting. The aim is to ensure the best translation for your recording, i.e., brings out the best possible sound. Mastering is an art that has its own set of approaches and techniques.

Advanced Techniques for Mastering

This section contains a wide array of techniques, some may be simple protocols to be observed, which are very crucial in your mastering processes, and some may help improve your work, while others prevent degradation. These techniques may be common or rare, but you can be able to choose what works for you and your music.

Minimizing delay between comparisons: there are instances when comparison will be made between an original version and a processed version, minimizing delay is important for absolute judgment. A common feature of DAW that helps you make a comparison is the solo mode. Particularly in mastering, the most common solo mode is exclusive, once you select exclusive and a track solo button is pressed, all other track will be un-soloed. But if the exclusive mode is not selected, a group of tracks is soloed, and this will not work if you are making an instant comparison.

How to avoid ear fatigue: Studies have shown that there are two types of ear fatigue, the short term and the long term. You can easily recover from short term ear fatigue under two minutes; this is why mastering engineers take short breaks in between sessions and before making any final decisions. Long term ear fatigue may be a result of long-term exposure to sound about 75dBSPL and above, so be careful not to expose your ears to such loudness.

Stem mastering: this is mastering performed from sub-mixes called the stem. The aim of stem mastering is to minimize some sacrifices made during mastering, for example, cutting or raising of bass frequencies only in the stem where the bass instrument is present instead of doing this for the entire mix. Stem mastering is a good option when the mastering environment is not conducive or when there are significant problems with no particular solution.

Reverb processing: Reverb should not be used on a professional production unless there is a need for significant depth. When you are working with this type of trouble mix, the first step is to try a remix, and if this does not work, you can add subtle high-quality reverb. The most basic way to approach this is to use a reverb processor coupled with a transient processor over the entire mix. This way, the punch will be intact with little reduction. In mastering, whenever Reverb is to be used, the reverb pre-delay settings, which will delay the reverb signal, is adjusted to achieve the best result. Doing this will help reduce the masking of the main signal by the reverb signal.

Processing song section separately: earlier, we learned that mastering deals with the entire mix, so it involves finding settings that work for the entire song.

Sometimes a problem may arise in a particular section such that there will be a need for the said section to be processed separately. Sometimes, removing a single click or pop can lead to you destructively editing a small piece, probably even saving a new version of the change. The repair edits are often carried out in the waveform view of many DAWs. But if there is a problem with an entire section, it can be cut into separate parts and processed, after which you edit the parts back together; if the processing involves phase shift, it can lead to a problem in timing. This may be an anomaly in the beginning or end of an edit; careful editing can easily address this problem.

Reference recording: Reference recording are popular recordings of the highest quality with which is used for comparison with the recording being mastered. Most professionals have their own collection of reference recordings, or they can ask their clients to submit a reference recording that will give them insight into their client's taste. You can be able to capture your client's sonic vision through their reference recording; sometimes, it helps you reset your ear and perception while giving you a sense of balance. Reference recording can be an audio CD or a digital file that can be loaded into the DAW or played on a separate device. The best way to store a reference recording on the hard drive is through FLAC format. This will help preserve the original quality of the reference track.

Mono compatibility: it is crucial to listen to how your recording sounds when converted to mono. It has been said that listening to a recording with a car stereo is like listening to it in mono because of the arrangement of the speaker. Many DAWs and mastering console comes with features that enable you to listen to your recording in mono.

Chapter Eleven: Manufacture and Distribution/Format

The Digital World in Music

The digital world has played a major role in the music industry. The ever-evolving technology has changed the way music is manufactured and distributed today. It facilitates the means of producing and distributing music at a low cost. Nowadays, it is easier to produce music in the comfort of your room with just simple equipment, all thanks to digital technology.

Multimedia and Web

Nowadays, the modern-day computers are much faster with multi-functional abilities. Not only do they make our work easier, but they have also been able to integrate media and networking into their functions as well. But in the real sense, multimedia is a unified programming and operating system. This system allowed multiple forms of program data to be stream and routed simultaneously to the appropriate hardware port for processing.

Delivery Media

In media, data can be transmitted over a wide range of storage device; there are three major delivery media:

CD

This compact disk is one of the important formats used in the distribution and marketing of music. It is in two forms, CD-ROM and CD-audio. The CD-ROM is capable of storing

700mb of graphics, digital audio, text, and raw data while its audio counterpart can store up to 74 minutes of audio.

DVD

They are capable of storing up to 8.5 gigabytes of data on the double-layer disc and about 4.7 gigabytes on the single-sided disc. This capacity makes it the perfect delivery medium for DVD-Audio. They can contain any form of data.

Web

One major aspect of multimedia is the ability to transmit data or information to either an individual or to the masses. And this is achieved through a network connection. The largest and common connection is the connection to the internet. The internet is a complex communication system that allows your computer to be connected to the internet service provided while an internet browser transmits and receives information via a uniform resources locator address.

Audio Format

The delivery format is very important, especially when you are creating content for the media system. Your bandwidth requirement and format should be compatible with your content delivery system. Some of the formats of delivery are outlined below;

Uncompressed sound file format: they are bulky and occupies large space on your hard disk or any storage drive, but the main advantage of this format is that it maintains the quality of the digital audio stored on it, in other words, the quality of your audio remains unchanged no matter the number of times you process or encode it. An example of this is WAV format, AIFF format.

Compressed sound file format: one main advantage it has over the uncompressed format is that it makes more space available on your hard drive or any storage device, this is because it compresses the digital audio data leading to small file, but a major disadvantage is that it can lead to loss of data. The compressed sound file format can further be classified into two groups:

Lossless compressed audio format: in this format, your digital audio file is compressed to a smaller file, but the compression process does not result in loss of data or degradation in audio quality. A good example of this is the FLAC format.

Lossy compressed audio format: this format compress digital audio data, but the process eliminates some information and frequency to reduce the size. This results in a reduction of quality, which can be large or small depending on the amount of data that was eliminated. Subsequent processing will lead to more data loss. An example of this is MP3.

Commonly Used Audio Format

WAV format: This stores uncompressed audio data with 100% data quality retention. It is mainly based on the RIFF bitstream format of storing data since it retains the original quality of data; it is popular among audio experts, and also editing can be done using software and commonly used on Windows systems.

AIFF (Audio interchange file format) Format: was developed by Apple computers and can also store uncompressed audio data, commonly used on the Apple Macintosh system, this format is also popular among professionals.

MP3 format: this format reduces the size of a file by eliminating some information through psychoacoustic compression and perspective audio coding. It can retain a larger percentage of the quality of the original data. It is commonly used to store a large number of songs on the computer as it will not take up much space but never record in MP3 unless there is absolutely no other option. Always make sure your recording is in an uncompressed format like WAV or AIFF, you may decide to convert it to MP3 format.

FLAC (Free Lossless Audio Codec): this format reduces the size of your audio file but still maintains the quality of the original data.

AAC (Advanced Audio Format): unlike its MP3 counterpart, it offers better quality than the MP3 at a smaller size. It is the audio format being used by Apple's iTunes.

WMA (window media Audio) format: in this format, you can encode high-quality audio at a reduced size. A major advantage of this format is that it is able to reproduce the original quality with no elimination of data similar to WAV.

How do I choose the best recording format?

In choosing the best recording format, there are two factors to consider, sampling rate and bit rate.

Sampling rate: this is the number of samples received per second. Audio signals are broken into samples that are received by your device e.g., computer during recording. The sampling rate is measured in hertz; it allows you to listen to uninterrupted audio playback. The higher the sampling rate, the greater the audio quality. The standard sampling rate for CD is 44.1 kHz.

Bit rate: the number of bits processed per unit of playback time is referred to as bit rate. While the sample rate represents the number of samples recorded overtime, bit rate represents the quality of each individual sample recorded. The higher the bit rate, the higher the quality of your audio, but the larger space it will occupy on your hard drive. Most studio prefers their bit rate to be 24, 32 or more; this is because there is more accuracy with your data, and this important for mixing and mastering process.

Surround Sound

Surround sound started in the theatre; incorporating this technique into your speaker system will help enrich the depth and fidelity of your sound. Surround sound is designed to create a sound filed around you and also able to recreate the sound above you.

Ideally, a surround sound is made up of five speakers and a subwoofers, and if the room is long, then it requires seven speakers and a subwoofers, three speakers are installed along the front wall; one to the right, one to the left and the other at the center, one or two pairs of speakers are installed at the rear wall, thereby surrounding you with sound in all direction.

Monitor Placement in Surround Sound

The monitor of choice for your surround sound depends on the level of quality, functionality, and cost. All these factors must be taken into account before choosing a monitor. Another important factor to consider is how you plan to monitor in surround. Does your console or DAW offer true monitor surround capabilities? If they do, then you are lucky, and if they don't, you will need a hardware surround monitor control system or a surround preamp. Take your time to research and decide the type of surround mastering tool that will be best for your music; Mixing and mastering in surround can be a real challenge, when you considered all the factors and have made your decision, you can then go ahead to install a 5.1 surround system.

The 5.1 monitor set-up is made-up of five full-range speakers arranged in a circular arc with the speakers at equal distance from a center position. Three speakers at the front, as explained earlier with the center speaker being placed at dead center 00 from the center point and the other two (the one on the left and right) being placed at 300 arcs of the speaker at the center. The remaining two are at 1100at the rear from the center point. The subwoofer should be placed near the dead center. Also, active subwoofers offer full control over gain and crossover frequency. All the surround monitors should be gain-adjusted in order to be able to deliver the same sound output level.

The surround system makes use of bass management to low route frequency to the subwoofers. The subwoofers channel is called ".1" because the range is limited to bass frequency alone. A major advantage of bass management is that it takes much load off the speakers, so they can sound louder with little to no distortion as they don't have to produce bass frequencies.

Chapter Twelve: Predictions

Through the years, sound technology has improved and is still improving. Two modern factors that have come into play are digital audio and the web. The ability to turn the digital 1's and 0's into alphabetical words has been a turning point that has changed communication and creative production.

The advent of pc, DAWs, and digital downloads has not only made music production easy and cost-effective, but it also creates certain flexibility and an ideal environment for music production. Beyond all this is the World Wide Web; this has taken music to a new height. Music is not static; it is growing and evolving every day.

Music in the last few decades has witnessed the advent of file sharing to the invention of DAWs. But in the next coming decade, it would still undergo some more transformation. A few decades ago, before you can become an international star, you need a huge record label, millions of investment and still look the part, but nowadays, a lot of stars are born through the internet, and in the next couple of decades more stars will be born through this. This is because the internet, social media smartphone, coupled with internet speed streaming, will put a lot of artists into the limelight without the help of a record label. In the near future, record labels may be a thing of the past; the main function of a record label is marketing, distribution, and A&R.

In the past, labels would discover an artist and develop them to become a global sensation, but now the A&R function of a record label is being eradicated as artists are now signed on the strength of their streaming or social media followers, where there is an existing fan base for the label to utilize. Nowadays, there is little need for a record label in the distribution of music; anyone can distribute their music through a digital service provider for a token. It does not mean that record labels are not required; getting signed to a record label has its own advantage and privileges, but in the near future, there might not be a need for them anymore. Autonomous artists!

Soon, music will become more global and more localized, in the sense that more audiences would have access to music, even ones that are not in their original language. Meanwhile, artists who previously felt obliged to perform in English will start performing in their original language.

Soon, Artificial intelligence is going to be a turning point for the music industry, in fact, they are already changing it, with tools like A.I- mediated composition and voice synthesis, thousands of musician all over the world will be able to produce high-quality music by themselves and distribute at a lower cost.

Conclusion

Before you can become a professional, you must have been a beginner at one point. At the beginner stage of your journey, you must have been on shaky ground, but transcending into a professional is all about solidifying and legitimizing your stance in the whole scheme of things, music production-wise, of course. A beginner who is ready to go pro must have acquired the necessary tools, technical knowhow, financial, and mental ability to be able to go the extra mile.

The assumption under which this book is compiled is that you already have considerable knowledge about what music production is all about, especially if you were opportune to read the beginner edition. Therefore, if the book was not basic enough for your taste, I apologize profusely. I tried as much as possible not to dictate/enforce exactly what to buy and use in terms of studio equipment, both hardware, and software, but rather provide information on the attributes you should look out for so that you have the opportunity to derive what works best for you.

A few of the issues tackled in the book are as follows but are not limited to it.

☐ The components of a professional music studio.

☐ The pro-DAW system.

☐ Professional music capable home recording studio.

☐ How a studio is to be designed.

☐ The importance of working together (collaboration).

☐ The importance of soundproofing.

☐ The rudiments of Acoustic treatment.

☐ Explicit discussion on some of the instruments used in the studio

☐ Professional roles in music production

☐ Structure and arrangement of hit songs

☐ The production process

☐ Predictions on what to expect in 2020, and many more.

A lot of emphases were made in the book about the importance of initially establishing both your long term and short-term goals, so you have a clear path to achieving them. Doing this makes you more focused, which increases the probability of you achieving your aims. The book also advocated that you should have a mentor (an authority in professional music production) whose footsteps you will adopt as a kind of blueprint to your own work.

Finally, in your struggle to attain professionalism, do not settle for just the ordinary or normal or status quo. Always strive to do your best at all times. Do not follow the trend blindly; rather, observe it and then manipulate it to suit your perspective. At the end of it all, your efforts will be crowned with the production of not just great recordings but unique ones too. Takes this advice with you as a parting gift; Practice and hard work are never too much. The so-called seasoned professional still make errors; therefore, what excuse do you have?

Discover "How to Find Your Sound"

http://musicprod.ontrapages.com/

Swindali music coaching/Skype lessons.

Email djswindali@gmail.com for info and pricing

References

https://www.renegadeproducer.com/music-production-techniques.html

https://www.musicradar.com/tuition/tech/19-sequencing-and-midi-power-tips-191594

https://www.audio-issues.com/home-recording-studio/demystifying-audio-formats-what-format-should-you-record-in/

https://www.musicradar.com/tuition/tech/12-sound-layering-tips-and-tricks-589568

https://www.waves.com/six-stages-of-music-production

https://en.m.wikipedia.org/wiki/Mixing_engineer

https://www.careersinmusic.com/

https://www.techwalla.com/articles/the-difference-between-subwoofers-speakers

https://musiccritic.com/equipment/speakers/10-best-studio-monitors-speakers/

https://iconcollective.edu/best-studio-desks/

https://www.musiciansfriend.com/thehub/audio-mixers-how-to-choose

https://www.musiciansfriend.com/thehub/usb-microphone-buying-guide

https://www.thebalancecareers.com/what-is-a-sound-engineer-2460937

https://www.tunecore.com/blog/2018/05/how-to-write-produce-hit-song-in-2018.html

https://www.hitsongsdeconstructed.com/

Using a professional music recording studio can make a difference in your career, here's why

https://www.tunedly.com/blogpost?blog=WhyUseaProRecordingStudio?

The recording engineer and other roles found in the studio

https://www.practical-music-production.com/recording-engineer/

How to collaborate effectively with other music producers

https://www.izotope.com/en/learn/how-to-collaborate-effectively-with-other-music-producers.html#person

Collaboration: how your music can benefit from producing with others

https://www.edmprod.com/collaboration/

How to soundproof a room for audio recording

https://www.adorama.com/alc/how-to-soundproof-a-room-for-audio-recording

How to soundproof a room for music (Listening and Recording)

https://aquietrefuge.com/soundproof-room-for-music/

Music Collaboration: How-To and Why

https://www.musicgateway.com/blog/how-to/music-collaboration-how-to-best-music-collaboration-sites

How to build a recording studio

https://www.planetarygroup.com/music-promotion-guide/build-recording-studio/

Top 10 DAW recording software 2020

https://musiccritic.com/equipment/software/best-daw-recording-software/

Audio production

https://www.audiomentor.com/audioproduction/how-to-choose-a-daw

The acoustic treatment for panels & foam

https://ledgernote.com/columns/studio-recording/acoustic-treatment-guide-for-panels-and-foam/

The complete recording studio equipment list

https://ehomerecordingstudio.com/recording-studio-equipment-list/

Modern Recording Techniques 7th and 8th editions by David Miles Huber

The Music Business and Recording Industry 3rd Edition by Geoffrey P. Hull, Thomas Hutchison, and Richard Strasser.

The Mixing Engineer's Handbook 3rd edition by Robby Owsinski.

Modern recording techniques by David Miles Huber

Home recording for musicians for dummies by Jeff Strong

Complete guide to audio mastering by Gebre Waddell

The mixing engineer's handbook by Bobby Owinski

CPSIA information can be obtained
at www.ICGtesting.com
Printed in the USA
LVHW020255141120
671607LV00005B/206